Mary Spencer Warren

The Princess of Wales

A biographical sketch

Mary Spencer Warren

The Princess of Wales
A biographical sketch

ISBN/EAN: 9783337012038

Printed in Europe, USA, Canada, Australia, Japan

Cover: Foto ©Raphael Reischuk / pixelio.de

More available books at **www.hansebooks.com**

THE PRINCESS OF WALES

A Biographical Sketch

BY

MARY SPENCER WARREN

WITH 53 ILLUSTRATIONS

LONDON
GEORGE NEWNES, LTD.
SOUTHAMPTON STREET, STRAND
1895

TO THE READER

I send this forth as the first published volume giving any account of the life of her Royal Highness the Princess of Wales, and making no pretence of eloquence in portraiture, I rely on the reader's indulgence for simplicity of narrative.

MARY SPENCER WARREN

CONTENTS

CHAPTER IV. 1863–1865

CHAPTER V. 1865–1868

CHAPTER VI. 1868–1870

PART II

CHAPTER I

CHAPTER II

CHAPTER III

H.R.H. THE PRINCE OF WALES

From a Photo. by W. & D. Downey

THE PRINCESS OF WALES

CHAPTER I

THERE are numbers of people whose lives never come in contact with our Royal family ; whose knowledge of their daily lives is, as it were, " a tale that is told." They hear of one member going here, and another going there, for some public or social event, but there their knowledge ends ; while the significance of the continual journeying to and fro is not often taken into consideration, and the large amount of good that is the result of this restless activity is not always apparent to those who are not directly interested in the functions. Others may be living in the midst of such a whirl of social life, that events in which they have perhaps

A

taken a prominent part fade imperceptibly from the mind, and sink into a shadowy past. From various causes, I am hopeful that these pages will prove an attractive whole to all classes of the community.

THE KING OF DENMARK
From a Photo. by Steen & Co., Copenhagen

It is scarcely possible to form any adequate idea of the large amount of beneficent assistance the Princess of Wales has rendered to all classes since she came to us, to be one with us and one of us. Ever ready and ever willing, she has worked with untiring zeal and unflagging exertion for the welfare of all classes of society, and England feels the gratitude she delights to show on every possible occasion.

Her Royal Highness Alexandra Caroline Maria Charlotte Louise Julie, Princess of Schleswig-Holstein, Sonderburg, Glücksburg—born December 1, 1844—was the eldest daughter and second child of Christian (younger brother of the Duke Charles who was head of a branch of the House of Holstein) and Louise Wilhelmina Friederike Caroline Auguste Julie, second daughter of William, Landgraf of Hesse-Cassel.

The Duke of Schleswig-Holstein, Sonderburg, Glücksburg was not in direct succession to the throne; and when he became Crown Prince of Denmark he stepped into a position which he had neither expected nor desired, but the duties of which he discharged with the faithful thoroughness which distinguished all his actions.

It was in 1842 that the Prince and Princess Christian were married, the ceremony taking place at Copenhagen, in the Gŭle Palais, situated in the street called the Amaliegade ; this street running right into the Amalien-borg Square, where the Royal Palaces are situated. The one in Amaliegade, where the marriage ceremony was performed, then became the home of the Prince and Princess, and here each of their children were born.

THE QUEEN OF DENMARK
From a Photo. by Steen

Sixteen years afterwards the Prince was proclaimed Heir Apparent, and received for himself and heirs the title of Royal Highness.

The entire population of Denmark at that

time was only 1,600,551; of Copenhagen only 155,143. The standing army of the country was 6000; and a navy of 97 vessels all told, carrying 1144 guns.

GŬLE PALAIS, AMALIEGADE
Where the Princess of Wales was born

In the early part of 1894 I was in Copenhagen, and then had the opportunity of seeing the Palaces, and making myself familiar with their interiors and contents. As the birthplace of our Princess, and the present home of her parents, a digression bearing upon them will be readily excused.

The Palace in which the Princess was

THE BALL-ROOM—AMALIENBORG
From a Photo. by Gunn & Stuart

born is comparatively small and unpretentious in appearance, and the street in which it stands is so quiet that more than once I walked down it when there was not a single individual in sight. It is, however, the very centre of the aristocracy of the place.

Previous to 1794, when Christian VII. was King, the royal residence was the

THE DRAWING-ROOM—AMALIENBORG
From a Photo. by Gunn & Stuart

Christianborg Palace, near the present site of the Railway Station. In that year a terrible fire broke out, and the really fine palace was almost totally destroyed. Here let me remark that fire has been a great

enemy to the Danish monarchy. I suppose
the ruins were practically beyond redemption,
for they have never been restored, but
'stand, one huge skeleton pile, almost the
first object on which the eye rests when
Copenhagen is reached.

Burned out of his town residence, then,
the King bought four small palaces which
had been built some years before by four
Danish nobles. One of these palaces contains
what is known as the State Apartments;
two others are occupied by the King and
Crown Prince; while the fourth is used as
the Foreign Office.

Here I may say a few words concerning
the King and Queen. The genial, kindly
nature of the King is well known; and it is
for this, quite as much as for the great strides
his country has made under his rule, that he
is so much beloved by his subjects. On
account of his age he is now prohibited from
the activity in public questions he formerly displayed, but though living a somewhat retired
life, he is a familiar figure in the streets of

the capital, and on several occasions I met him walking quietly along, quite unattended, looking with interest into the various shops, or stopping now and again to gaze at anything going on around him—always acknowledging the respectful salutations with which he was greeted. His Majesty shows a remarkable activity for his age, which he carries so well that few would believe him to be between seventy and eighty.

Her Majesty the Queen is remarkably gifted in many ways. With the extremely useful education which was imparted to her daughters all are familiar. The Princess of Wales' good taste and remarkable needle-work abilities seem to have been inherited, as her Majesty the Queen is much gifted in the same direction. The Queen is also a skilful and cultivated musician, being a good pianist and a harpist of more than ordinary ability. Whenever she has the opportunity, her great delight is to take part in harp trios, either with professional players or skilful amateurs. She is, of course, considerably advanced in years, but, like her husband, she is so extremely active in her movements that her appearance would lead one to believe her much younger.

It is admitted on all sides that this King and Queen are a remarkable couple; they and their family being certainly destined to become prominent figures in the world's history. One of their sons occupies the throne of Greece; another will in due course succeed to the throne of his father; one daughter was, until recently, for many years Empress of Russia; and still another is likely to occupy in the future what may be justly termed the most powerful throne in the world—the throne of England—although we hope that future may be far ahead; one of their grandchildren has just lately been proclaimed an Emperor; while still a larger number of these grandchildren will occupy similar eminent positions.

If anything were wanted to show the universal popularity of these monarchs, the cele-

bration of their Golden Wedding amply sup-
plied the want. On that occasion congratulations and presents poured in from nearly all
quarters of the world. The festivities connected with the event lasted for a week;
comprising audiences, receptions, State
dinners, balls, and a public thanksgiving
service at the church, to which all the royal
personages, ambassadors, and envoys went
in procession. In the palace may be seen
many of the presents given at the time : some
are highly valuable and valued; one is a
very handsome frame containing the portraits of the King and Queen and their
descendants ; and one a golden wreath subscribed for by 100,000 schoolchildren. Special features of the celebration were the
immense number of free dinners given to the
poor all over the King's dominions, and the
creation of one or two special charities from
sums freely subscribed for the purpose.

Then there is the Palace of Fredensborg, of
which we have heard much ; it is the favourite
summer residence of their Majesties, situated

in a magnificent park some few miles from the city. Here, nearly every autumn, the entire family are wont to gather, going from

ROSENBORG CASTLE

From a Photo. by Gunn & Stuart

England, Russia, Greece and Gmunden, to meet and spend a few happy weeks in an unconventional manner ; putting on one side all State duties and cares, partaking in

all manner of outdoor exercises, and enjoying
to the full all the ordinary indoor amusements
of a happy family party.

When I was at Fredensborg it was unfortunately dressed in brown holland, and but
little could be seen of the many beautiful
things contained in its rooms ; but everywhere are evidences of thoughtful affection
from various members of this large and united
family. Here is the library, well stocked
with a careful and valuable selection from
the best authors past and present. Here,
too, is her Majesty's boudoir, crowded with
portraits of children, grandchildren, and great-
grandchildren, and curios and articles, dear
for their associations, sent from many
countries.

Also, I went over the Schloss Rosenborg ;
which was founded by Christian IV. in 1604.
In it I saw very much that was extremely interesting, and also highly instructive. Going
from room to room one sees the varied posses-
sions of the different monarchs ; showing the
progress of civilisation and education, and the

consequent advance of every art and science. In the Knights' Hall, or Riddersal, the principal objects are the Coronation chairs, which stand at the northern end.   Over the seats

THE ROSE—ROSENBORG

From a Photo. by Gunn & Stuart

is a velvet canopy, the seats themselves being of fabulous wealth.   That of the King consists almost entirely of ivory of the narwhale, and shows several allegorical figures. On the summit is placed a ball, under which on Coronation-day may be seen an amethyst, said to be the largest known ; this, for safety, however, is kept in the Regalia Room, which opens on the right of this hall. This I found to be a veritable strong-room, the contents of which are not even to be gazed upon by ordinary individuals. I should not like to venture any idea of the worth of this collection, containing, as it does, articles of great value from the commencement of the Oldenberg dynasty. The walls are hung with Oriental tapestry which is used at coronations. Amongst the numerous costly objects I noticed the State sword of Christian III.; the crown of Christian IV., enamelled, embossed and chased, and studded with diamonds ; the original Orders of the Danneborg and the Elephant ; Christian IV.'s sword used by him for conferring knighthood ; various gold vessels and crown diamonds, the orb and sceptre ; and the crowns of the present King and Queen.

Re-entering the Riddersal, I noticed, on my right, the Danish royal christening font, which is of siver-gilt beautifully embossed. It was in this font that our Princess and each of her brothers and sisters were baptized.

CHRISTENING FONT OF DANISH ROYAL FAMILY

It stands on a small piece of Oriental carpet, perfectly unique in its design, and said to be almost priceless.

The Palace of Bernstorff is another

favourite residence of the family. Here, when Crown Prince and Princess, they passed the summer months ; and the annual autumn gatherings have occasionally been held here.

Copenhagen itself is a first-rate business centre, having a good opera-house, some fine churches and hospitals, a large observatory, many imposing warehouses, several fine streets of good shops, where all sorts of articles quite up to date may be purchased. In and around the city are some good walks and drives, on one side of it being a pretty park, through which one may stroll away to the fine promenade in front of the sea. The docks are large, and exceptionally fine ; day after day a busy scene is enacted there, for vessels are continually arriving and leaving. Altogether, Copenhagen is extremely well worth a prolonged visit.

To return from the digression, and resume at the period when the Prince and Princess Christian were residing partly at the house I have named, near the Royal Palace, and partly in the suburbs.

Many romantic accounts have been given
of the Prince having to supplement his income by giving drawing lessons; but this is
altogether contrary to fact. Most certainly
the Prince had only a small private fortune,
and his income from the Rigsdag was not of
large dimensions; so that partly owing to
this, and partly to a natural love of retirement, the Prince and Princess led a very
quiet and unpretentious existence, devoting
themselves to their children's education and
welfare, and earning golden opinions from
the poor for the charitable assistance and
kindly sympathy they rendered them.

The daughters of the Prince and Princess
were brought up in the simplest manner.
Much of their education was conducted by
their parents, and was thorough in the
extreme. Thoroughly practical it was too,
the useful taking predominance over the
ornamental. Undoubtedly it was a fact that
many of the dresses which the Princesses
wore were made by themselves. At the
same time the father and mother took very

good care that their daughters should be trained so as to adorn any future exalted position which they, as Royal Princesses, might be called upon to occupy. Honesty of purpose in all things was the lesson that the parents ever placed before their children, and no one who has watched these children grow up can ever say that the lesson failed in its application.

THE PRINCESS, 1861
From a Photo. by Hansen, Copenhagen

There is really very little to tell about the early life of the Princess, by reason of the perfectly unostentatious manner in which her time was passed.

Her Royal Highness was not yet seventeen years of age when she first met the Prince of Wales. Various accounts are given of this meeting, and the manner in which it was brought about. One tells how the Prince, quite by accident, saw her photograph ; and commissioned the holder of the photograph to visit Denmark to open up negotiations with the parents of the Princess whose face had charmed him. Another tale goes, that the two met by accident on the Continent, where an attachment sprang up between them. I think I may claim that the following account may be regarded as trustworthy. The Prince of Wales had heard—as had many other people—of the beauty of the daughters of the Prince and Princess Christian. Of course the only one of a marriageable age was the eldest, Princess Alexandra. It was arranged, then, that as the two families would be travelling on the Continent during the ensuing year, a meeting should take place in order that they might make each other's acquaintance, with a view to marriage, should the meeting result in a mutual affection. Both were staying at Worms, and the first meeting was really accidental ; for, while inspecting the Cathedral,

they met and were introduced. This interview was brief, but of sufficient duration for
the Prince to become deeply enamoured of
the lovely face and graceful bearing of her
who afterwards became his consort.

The prelimin-
aries of the alliance
were settled in the
autumn of 1862,
when her Majesty
the Queen was on
the Continent for
a short visit, and
in November of the
same year her
Royal Highness
paid a visit to
Osborne.

THE PRINCESS, 1863
From a Photo. by Bingham, Paris

Undoubtedly,
this match was one of mutual affection and
quite free from the political and State interests that often distinguish royal alliances.

Denmark was a country towards which the
English people were disposed to be very

friendly, the beauty and goodness ofthe young
Princess were becoming proverbial, so that
in all parts of the kingdom, with high and
low, rich and poor, the projected alliance
found favour ; and every one was on the *qui
vive* for the coming event.

CHAPTER II

THE treaty was duly signed on the 15th of January, 1863, and that was the signal for such an outburst of enthusiastic loyalty as has seldom, if ever, been witnessed even in loyal England.

In London, and in all parts of the country, meetings were held with the object of providing the most suitable reception of her Royal Highness on her arrival, and various modes of celebrating the happy event were arranged.

That Denmark was gratified goes without saying, and although the joy was marred by the approaching separation, yet the pride with which the people regarded their favourite, and the position she was about to take was unbounded; and each vied with the other in manifestations of loyalty, love, and good-will.

The sum of 100,000 kroners* was quickly subscribed as the peoples' dowry, and public and private presents poured in on every hand. First must be mentioned that of the King, which consisted of a diamond necklace, containing as centre-piece a fac-simile of the famous " Dagmar Cross."

THE PRINCESS, 1863
From a Photo. by Walker, London

Some of the farewells were touching in the extreme; for instance, such a one as took place on the Sunday, which was to be the last her Royal Highness would spend in the old palace previous

* Kroner, Danish, worth 1s. 8d.

to her departure for a new country and a new people. Quite a number of the poor had subscribed for the purchase of a very handsome pair of vases, and with the aged pastor at their head, a deputation proceeded thither to present them. With a voice faltering with emotion, the aged man, who had long ministered to the spiritual wants of the family, and had watched the growth of the youthful princess, spoke the words of farewell, and of good wishes and blessing for the future, an address to which her father, the Prince Christian, had almost as much difficulty in replying.

Our Princess on this occasion manifested the kindness and generosity of disposition for which she was already well known by giving a considerable sum of money to be divided amongst six poor brides who were to be married on the same day as herself.

At length arrived the momentous day on which the home with all its associations of youthful happiness must be left behind, and the shy girl of eighteen must face the world of criticism, and the unknown life before her.

Escorted by father, mother, brothers, and sisters, and attended by Danish officials of high rank, her Royal Highness commenced her journey.

Everywhere, from Copenhagen to Brussels, the popularity of the Princess was unbounded. Every railway station, and every inch of road was lined with crowds of people; decorations, illuminations, torchlight processions, military, instrumental, and vocal music all contributing to the impressiveness of the occasion.

Meanwhile, England had made preparations on a costly and expensive scale; money was spent lavishly. The approaching marriage was the all-absorbing topic, and the country was stirred to the utmost pitch of excitement. In castle and cottage, counting-house and workshop, the event was looked forward to; and if ever

London lost its usual business tone and appearance, it was surely at this time.

Many clamoured for the solemnisation of the marriage ceremony in London, but as no one of our Chapels Royal could give sufficient accommodation for the large number that must inevitably be invited, it was wisely decided it should take place at Windsor, where the space would be of great advantage, the historic associations, costly architecture, and heraldic display being calculated in every way to add to the dignity and grandeur of the imposing scene.

London, however, was not to be left out ; and if it could not turn out *en masse* to shout its huzzas for the wedding, it found ample solace in the assurance that the Princess Alexandra would pass through from one end to another, in company with her future husband. The city was transformed into a veritable fairy-land, triumphal arches, flags, evergreens, mottoes, and everything in the way of decorations that man could devise, appeared at every point; every roof, every window, and every available inch of ground was utilised, and the entire seven miles of the route presented an appearance never to be forgotten by the thousands who were fortunate enough to see it.

England had not witnessed the marriage of a Prince of Wales for sixty-seven years, and the present Prince was the son of a Queen and mother who was good and popular; and who moreover had been recently so sadly bereaved as to have the lively sympathy of the nation at large. The Prince of Wales was not yet much known in public, but the people were ready to accept him as the son of wise and good parents, knowing that by them he had been carefully trained for the high position in which he was destined to move. Report said that the youthful Princess so soon to be his bride was as good as she was beautiful, so that altogether the magnitude of the welcome could scarcely excite wonder, or the fact that, as one noble writer of the time said : "All London went mad over the marriage." All business cares and duties were placed completely in the background, and the whole population gave themselves up unreservedly to the one event.

It is reported that a crowd equal to more than five times the population of Copenhagen waited patiently in London streets for upwards of six hours, in order to catch a fleeting glimpse of her for whom this splendid welcome was prepared. Many who had paid large sums for windows or seats took up their position the night before, or very early in the morning; while numbers who neglected this necessary precaution never reached their desired haven, but, getting firmly wedged at some point which they did not desire, had to content themselves with a view of military helmets, horses' heads, the sound of deafening cheers, a general sense of being mangled and suffocated, and perhaps a journey home hatless, and with only the remnants of coat or mantle ;

and, as cabs were at a premium, and omni-
buses scarce, many had to traverse long
distances looking as nearly as possible as
though they had just taken part in a riot
or free fight.

CHAPTER III

As I have before intimated, Gravesend was the place selected for the Princess to disembark, and the little town was not at all in the background with regard to the warmth of the welcome; for preparations were made with a result that did all concerned the utmost credit. Everybody who was anybody was at the landing-stage in anxious expectation and brave attire; one special feature was the group of sixty fair maids of Kent dressed in white, waiting with baskets of choice flowers to cast on the pathway of the young girl, who was now emerging from a life of seclusion to one of the most brilliant positions the world could offer.

The Royal yacht *Victoria and Albert* had been placed at the disposal of Her Royal

Highness, and that vessel, together with an imposing escort of eight British men-of-war, had proceeded up the Channel in brilliant style.

Just as the yacht steamed in, the signal was given that His Royal Highness the

VICTORIA AND ALBERT YACHT

Prince of Wales had arrived at Gravesend Railway Station on his way to meet his bride; and not many minutes had elapsed before he was on board, eager to meet and welcome her to whom he had given his best affections. Rather a trying moment

for both, with so many curious eyes looking
on! The Prince was certainly equal to the
occasion, for advancing quickly to the door
of the state cabin, where the Princess stood
waiting for him, he took both her hands
into his, and imprinted an affectionate kiss
on her lips. It was the " one touch of nature
that makes the whole world kin," for matrons
and maids smiled approval, and young men
and old men burst out with hearty "bravos"
and cheers, and with not a few, handkerchiefs came into immediate requisition.

The Prince had now to meet the greater
part of his intended bride's family for the
first time. That he found favour in their
eyes, and that he became then, as he has
continued to be ever since, an immense
favourite with all, is a certainty.

Some of the Danish family were so eager
to see the long-talked of England that, not
waiting for the moment of disembarkation,
they proceeded to the upper deck, and there
viewed with wonder the impressive scene.
Bands played, guns fired, people shouted

themselves hoarse, and a general air of jubi-
lation sat on all when Her Royal Highness
the Princess Alexandra, leaning on the arm
of her future husband, at length stepped on
to the landing-stage at Gravesend. Of the
presentation of bouquets and addresses, it is
not necessary to do more than make passing
mention. I can well leave all this to the
imagination of my readers, as the sort of
thing is continually repeating itself.

Now all could see for themselves that the
reports of the beauty of Her Royal Highness
had not been one whit exaggerated, but
rather that the reality surpassed the rumour.
One smile from the beautiful face quickly
won every heart, and commencing on that
spot, gathering in volume on the journey
right through to Windsor, and swelling and
continuing to this year of grace 1895, one
harmonious chorus of praise was, and is, the
universal tribute to Alexandra, " England's
Princess."

The special train in which the journey to
London was made, was driven by the Earl

of Caithness, who, proud of his charge, drove his engine slowly up, in order that the people assembled at the different stations, and even along parts of the line, could get just a fleeting view.

The scene at Bricklayer's Arms Station was imposing in the extreme. Right well and loyally had the company done their share in the day's proceedings. Here a brief halt was made, and a necessary luncheon partaken of.

Words would fail me to describe the appearance of the streets ; but when I say that the first decorative talent of the day had been called into requisition, and that the City alone spent about £10,000 in embellishing itself, some idea of the magnificent display can be gathered.

But all sank into insignificance besides the countless thousands of people who had waited so long and so patiently for the sight of the young, fair face now before them ! Probably never had the verdict of the people been so unanimous. All with one accord and with

one voice shouted such a hearty, loyal greeting as I venture to say lives still in the
memory of the gracious lady for whom it was
given.

Well might the Prince look smiling and
happy, for clearly his choice was the people's
choice, and proclaimed so in no unmistakable
tone.

As the cortége proceeded through the
City, the crowds grew — if possible — still
more dense, and the display more imposing ;
and one can scarcely wonder that the Princess
showed occasionally the astonishment she felt,
while some of the Danish Ministers stood up
in their carriages in surprise.

At several points it was all but impossible
to proceed ; indeed, more than once the
carriages came to a complete standstill.

It is much to be wondered at that accidents
were not more numerous, and many were
only prevented with the utmost difficulty and
most strenuous exertions. At, and near, the
Mansion House the pressure was so great
that several became entangled in the wheels

of the different carriages, and the young
Princess was seen more than once to lean
over, and with her own hands help to dis-
entangle the heads of some venturesome
youths from the wheels of her own carriage.
Not particularly clean, and not particularly
inviting at all in appearance, were these
same youths; and when the solicitude of Her
Royal Highness for the very poorest and
lowliest was seen the enthusiasm knew no
bounds. Soldiers and police combined had
to use all their power to prevent the people
taking the horses out, and dragging the carriage in triumph on its journey. And surely
the Princess could not but be touched at the
honest, hearty tribute paid to her that day by
all sorts and conditions of men! It must
have been a wonder to many how she bore it
all so well, how mile after mile, and hour after
hour, her noble dignity and sweet frank smile
met all eyes; and her graceful acknowledg-
ments of the evidence of the people's trust in
her never wearied. Said one burly country-
man : " I have come all the way from Carlisle

to see her, and I would stand here in the
rain till this time to-morrow if I could only
set eyes on that bonny face again."

"Bless her heart," said a stout matron;
"I hope the Queen will give her a right
motherly welcome. Do you think she'll kiss
her?"

"I know I would if I were the Queen,"
answered another.

And so amid acclamations, blessings, and
prayers, the youthful pair—so soon to unite
their lives—passed through the midst of the
English people, and were taken, as it were,
to their hearts.

The same hearty demonstration occurred
throughout the journey, but the programme
was diversified slightly by a large force of
Volunteers being drawn up in Hyde Park on
either side of the carriage-way down which
the Prince and Princess were to proceed.
Our citizen soldiers were almost in their
infancy then, and the arrival of a young and
lovely princess was not an everyday affair,
so there was some excuse to be made for the

remarkable manner in which some of them acted. They gave the salute at command, and then, forgetting all discipline, broke their ranks and ran after the carriage.

Unfortunately, the rain, which had hitherto confined itself to two or three brief showers, came down heavily when Windsor was reached; that, and the lateness of the hour, owing to the length of time in crossing London, rather spoilt the effect of all the arrangements in the Royal borough; but I should imagine the Princess was thankful to reach the castle as quickly as possible, tired out as she must have been with the week of incessant travelling, the immense excitement, and the continuous and ever-changing scenes and faces, all so widely different from her former quiet and unpretentious life in the happy home circle.

The brilliant ceremony of the following Tuesday is a matter of history; for display of magnificent robes, priceless jewels, Court, military, and naval uniforms, it was superbly unique. All the best that art, beauty, and fashion could bring together, were beneath the roof of St. George's Chapel on the 10th of March, 1863. Quite early the invited guests were in their places, in anxious expectation of the various coming processions ; music of the best was discoursed to beguile the waiting minutes.

Presently the members of the Royal family commenced to arrive, and a goodly array there was of them, too! Her Majesty the Queen did not mingle with them round the altar on this occasion : her bereavement was too recent, and too sad a memory, for her to feel unalloyed joy ; so she occupied a private closet, or pew, above, where she could have a good view of the entire proceedings. You may be quite sure her mother's heart was in sympathy with the event, and if her joy *was* chastened, she could not but be glad for the happiness of her first-born son, and proud of his lovely bride, her daughter from this day.

If the Princess Alexandra had charmed everybody when she arrived in England,

WINDSOR CASTLE AND ST. GEORGE'S CHAPEL.

From a Photo. by Bedford Lemere

how much was the feeling increased now
when she swept in in her bridal array? I
shall not attempt a full description of the
various toilettes, but for the benefit of my
lady readers must just give a few particulars
of that worn by the Princess. The dress was
composed of Brussels lace, curiously wrought,
with groundwork of English crowns, and the
bride's initials, interspersed with which were
designs of roses, fuchsias, and forget-me-nots.
It was of great beauty and priceless in value,
and was the present of the King of the
Belgians. The bouquet was composed of
orange blossoms, white rosebuds, rare orchid
flowers, and sprigs of myrtle. The diamonds Her Royal Highness wore were the
gifts of the Prince of Wales, and of her
uncle.

As I have said, the appearance of the
Princess was lovely in the extreme, and as
she came up the aisle on the arm of her
father, followed by the eight beautiful and
high-born bridesmaids, murmurs of admiration—which even this well-bred audience

could not altogether suppress—was heard on every hand.

Well, the ceremony passed off much as the majority of fashionable weddings do, save for the additional brilliancy necessarily attending one of so great importance as this. There is one incident I cannot but place on record, and that is that the world-renowned Madame Goldsmid (Jenny Lind) was present in the special choir, and added her beautiful voice to the pæan of thanksgiving that was rendered on the occasion. Matchless songstress as she was, she deemed this a fitting event for sinking a voice that could entrance thousands to one of a choir ; and knowing that she was a truly good woman, we may be quite sure that when she mingled with others in rendering the beautiful words from the pen of His late Royal Highness Prince Albert it was no lip service, but an earnest and sincere prayer, embodied in the lines :

> " This day, with joyful heart and voice
> To Heav'n be raised a Nation's prayer;
> Almighty Father, deign to grant
> Thy blessing to the wedded pair."

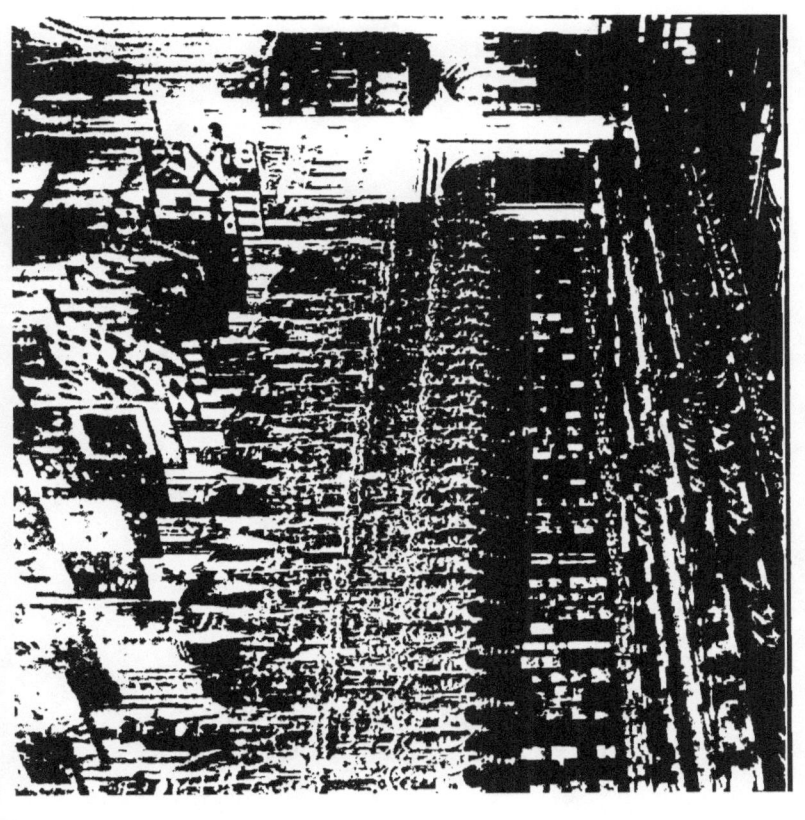

ST. GEORGE'S CHAPEL, WINDSOR

From a Photo. by Bedford Lemere

I can imagine how proud the parents of the Princess must have felt when they saw their child surrounded by so many ready to love her and welcome her as their own. Indeed, we are told that the handsome Prince Christian —now King of Denmark—and the Princess, his wife—almost as youthful-looking as her daughter—were " visibly proud and elated."

Of course there was the customary wedding breakfast, where speeches were made and responded to. But, better than all, in nearly every town and village throughout the country the poor were enabled to celebrate the event too : large sums of money had been collected, and dinners to some, and teas to others, were plentifully provided. In Copenhagen all the poor were feasted at the expense of the Crown, and everywhere, whether under the burning sun of India or in snowy Canada, wherever the Queen ruled the day was celebrated with many a joyous meeting, and millions of people were wishing " Long life and happiness to the Prince and Princess of Wales."

D

CHAPTER IV

It would take up too much time to tell you of all the presents, which were numerous and varied, and came from all parts of the land, and from all sorts and conditions of men and women. One of the most costly was the gift of the City of London—a diamond necklace of great beauty—which cost £10,000. One that I am sure the Princess would value very much—fond as she is of children—was a Bible and desk presented by the Sunday-schools of England. Some were noticeable partly from their associations—such as the priceless Irish lace from the ladies of Ireland and the Paisley shawl from the wives and daughters of the weavers of Paisley. It must have taken the Prince and Princess some time

to just look through them, as there were
sufficient to fill a museum. The public
were given an opportunity of examining
them, as they were afterwards placed on
view at the South Kensington Museum, and
attracted enormous crowds.

The honeymoon was spent at Osborne,
whither the Royal couple proceeded by
special train. On the way, at all the stations,
vast crowds had collected to see them pass.
At Reading a brief stoppage was made to
receive an address of respectful congratulation and the customary bouquets. A slight
and pleasing departure from the usual programme was made by the presentation of an
immense nosegay, on behalf of the poor of
the town, by an old woman upwards of seventy
years of age.

A large number of balls were given afterwards to celebrate the event, a notable
one being that of the Guards, given on the
26th of June, in the Picture Galleries of the
International Exhibition Buildings. It was
a scene of splendour such as one reads of

occasionally, but seldom sees. The plate
used for the event was computed to be worth
two millions sterling ; and everything else
was in the same costly and lavish style.
The guests present were of the very cream
of society, the number of invitations issued
having been limited to fourteen hundred.

Another was the one given by the City
Corporation, which was also a scene of
great splendour. Here a pleasant surprise
awaited the Princess in the Aldermen's
Court, consisting of a realistic moonlight
scene of the Palace of Bernstorff, artistically
designed and carried out, the Palace standing
out with sloping lawn and real flowers
and pathways ; on the lawn a figure of
the Princess herself. Needless to say her
Royal Highness was specially interested
and delighted with this unexpected represen-
tation of her former residence. The intense
love her Royal Highness bore for her home
would make the kind thoughtfulness of the
City magnates doubly appreciated.

The London season was a very brilliant

one, a vast impetus being given to trade in every direction. This was of course gratifying to all business men, as for some time everything had been very stagnant.

Sandringham—recently purchased for the Prince in accordance with the wishes of the late Prince Consort—was visited, her Royal Highness being much pleased with the pretty and quiet retreat, where there is such an abundance of wild and rural scenery. An exceedingly interesting reception was given to the Royal pair by the county families and villagers; huntsmen turning out in their scarlet and white, strewing choice flowers; and about two hundred schoolchildren, provided with flags, also strewing flowers. A reception this, such as the Princess would thoroughly enjoy, and that would remind her of the village scenes she had been wont to witness in Denmark.

Very soon her Royal Highness was following the bent of her inclination, and visiting the cottages and schools on the estate, suggesting improvements and altera-

tions here and there to ameliorate the condition of the poor, this being a subject in
which she has a very special interest, and
on no estate are labouring classes better
cared for than at Sandringham.

Various controversies had taken place as
to the selection of a London residence for
for the Prince and Princess.   Kensington
Palace and Marlborough House had both
been suggested.   Many thought the latter,
which had been erected in the time of
Queen Anne, and afterwards had served
as a picture gallery, was too diminutive
a residence for the heir to the throne and
his consort, but it was finally selected,
enlarged, and subjected to various alterations, and refurnished throughout.   Neither
Sandringham nor Marlborough House was
quite ready for them for a few months,
so they took up their temporary residence
at Frogmore, where they had a season of
rest and quiet after the various festivities.

Apart from these festivities, not many
public appearances were made, but one

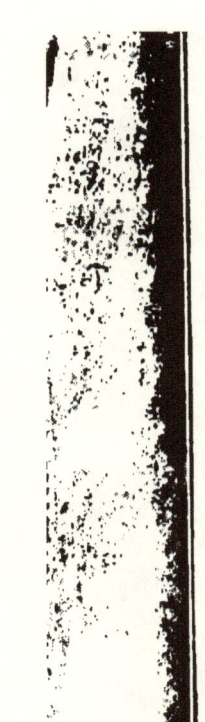

FRONT, MARLBOROUGH HOUSE

From a Photo.

great thing was done on behalf of the poor and destitute, and that was the inauguration of the new Orphan Asylum at Slough in June; this, being the first time that her Royal Highness had identified herself with any public cause, was an augury of what might be expected in the future from the charitable inclinations of the Princess.

In the same month the ceremony of inauguration of the Albert Memorial took place in the presence of the Prince and Princess: her Majesty having privately visited it some days previously.

Their Royal Highnesses also visited Oxford for two or three days, becoming the guests of Dean Liddell. While there they visited a bazaar for the benefit of the Infirmary, distributed prizes to the local volunteers, attended a Masonic ball and a grand banquet. During the whole time of their stay in the town, Oxford was *en fête*, and crowds were pouring in from every direction.

The volunteers at Wimbledon were also honoured with the presence of the Prince and Princess, who displayed much interest in the shooting.

On the 15th of November the Princess received tidings of the death of the King of Denmark, and the consequent accession of her father, Prince Christian, to the throne.

In the beginning of the next year (8th of January, 1864) the first Royal son was born at Frogmore Cottage. The Princess had been one of a skating party at Virginia Water that same day, and everybody was totally unprepared for such an event before March, consequently there was an utter dearth of official personages necessary for such a very important occurrence. One member of the Cabinet was present by the merest chance, happening to have gone down for a little shooting with the Prince. The doctors and the nurse could not possibly get there in time; and the public announcement was a huge surprise to the nation at large, although at the same time a source of unbounded satisfaction.

The infant Prince was christened on the

10th of March, being the anniversary of the marriage of the Prince and Princess; the ceremony taking place in the private chapel at Buckingham Palace, her Majesty the Queen being sponsor.

The responsibility of motherhood had now devolved upon the Princess, herself not much over nineteen years of age; the sequel will show how she accepted and fulfilled the duties of the sacred office.

Her Majesty's birthday was this year kept for the first time since the death of Prince Consort, and the citizens were gratified with not only the military "trooping of colours," always so impressive a ceremony, but also with the presence of their Royal Highnesses the Prince and Princess of Wales, when new colours were presented.

A volunteer review was also held at Hyde Park in presence of the Prince and Princess, the Prince taking part as colonel of his regiment. It was rather amusing, if a little unorthodox, but nevertheless a fact, that some of the officers saluting on the march past directed their looks, and equally of course their salutes, to the carriage in which her Royal Highness was seated, rather than to the Commander-in-Chief, who was on horseback near at hand.

That year, too, somewhat unexpectedly, the Prince and Princess went to Harrow for Speech Day. They had such a reception and such cheering in their honour as only schoolboys know how to give.

They also visited Cambridge, being received with great State by the Master of Trinity, together with dignitaries of the various colleges.

In July they visited the Horse Show at the Agricultural Hall; here they were expected some two or three days before they really went, but on the day in question no less than forty thousand people paid for admission. Indeed, it was remarkable what an immense concourse of people assembled every time the Prince and Princess were expected anywhere, and they were continually hailed with the most cordial expressions of goodwill. The beauty and winning smiles of the Princess charmed everybody with whom she came in contact, and the greatest efforts were made to catch even a remote glimpse of her.

In June the Prince and Princess were present at the headquarters of the Honourable Artillery Company, when the Princess presented new colours to this ancient regiment of the city of London.

In September the Prince and Princess embarked at Dundee for Denmark and Stockholm. Her Royal Highness was no doubt delighted at the thought of this home reunion, and the King and Queen would be just as pleased to welcome their dear daughter. Mother though the Princess was, she enjoyed some merry games with her sisters and brothers, and half lived the old life over again in their society.

Meanwhile, the Princess had not only made herself the admired of all classes of the community, but had proved herself to have become a "daughter more" to the Queen, who had indeed welcomed her as such in the first place. The Princess, with the tact that is a part of her nature, always did the right thing in the right place, and the two Royal ladies were as veritable mother and daughter. Her Royal Highness sought assiduously to cheer her august relative, and comfort her in her grief, which, from the peculiarity of her position, being compassed with affairs of State and the training of a family for a country's service, was not capable of being assuaged for a considerable period. Many would have wished to see her Majesty partly emerge from her retirement, and once more appear amongst her loyal subjects, and the Princess cordially endorsed this by her persuasive powers and loving attention. It is on record that on one occasion her Royal Highness, who is, as almost every one knows, the possessor of the rarest good taste, begged her Majesty to allow her to alter a certain heavily-craped bonnet which she was wearing. The Queen

after a time gave a reluctant consent, and
the result was that the Princess instantly
removed a quantity of the crape, and the
ladies present watching the effect saw the
bonnet, received by the Queen with a deep
sigh, and then an affectionate kiss. Sympathy and loyal affection drew tears from
more than one; but all were glad to notice
that the bonnet was worn. It was in little
acts such as this that the Princess endeared
herself to the Queen and every member of
the royal household.

Their Royal Highnesses were absent some
two months on their Danish visit, returning
to England refreshed and invigorated.

In the following June another son was
born — Prince George; this taking place
at Marlborough House; and one month
after an event occurred which but for the
promptness of His Royal Highness the
Prince of Wales might have had a very
different ending. It was on the 4th July
that suddenly an alarm was given that a
fire had broken out on the premises. After

E

some little delay it was found to be in the ventilating shaft running from the bottom to the top of the building. It was only the work of a few minutes to remove the Princess and her two boys—one an infant a month old—to the other side of the building, there to await for a short time the result of the efforts to be made for extinguishing the conflagration. The services of about fifty men-servants were quickly available, and placing himself at their head, minus his coat and waistcoat, the Prince worked as hard as any of them. Fearing at one time that the fire was getting to the roof, an ascent was made to explore, and here the Prince nearly came to grief, for accidentally putting his foot through the lath and plaster, he was only prevented just in time from going through the ceiling below. In the midst of it all one or two members of the Government happened to call, quite by accident, and had the edification of seeing the Prince in his shirt sleeves and much begrimed with smoke and dirt. Of course an alarm had been given at the nearest fire station—which institutions were not so numerous as now — and the men were on the spot as quickly as possible; by that time, however, the danger was nearly over. In the end the fire was got completely under, and the fire brigade men, as well as the royal servants, were entertained in the servants' hall. Great praise was due to the Prince for his prompt action, and also to the Princess for her courage and presence of mind under circumstances especially trying.

Another instance I can mention, that occurred very soon after, still further shows that our Princess is naturally of a courageous nature. This was the descent of the " Botallack " mine near the Land's End. This mine has a shaft two hundred fathoms deep. This for a lady is no ordinary feat, and most people would shrink from such an expedition. It was on a hot July morning when the Prince and Princess — the latter clad in a flannel dress, and straw hat trimmed with blue—went down to inspect the working. Very thoroughly they did their work too, for more than an hour went by before they reappeared on *terra firma*, looking, I am bound to confess, not any cleaner for the trip, and very hot; but Her Royal Highness was smiling as ever; and, to repeat her own words, "she had thoroughly enjoyed herself."

CHAPTER V

HER ROYAL HIGHNESS about this time paid her first visit to the Tower of London, this being of a private nature, with no special mounting of guard and Royal salutes. Some considerable time was spent in inspection of the armoury, ancient chapels, places of execution, and cells rendered historical by the statesmen and even Royal persons who had passed so many weary days in them. Our gentle and kindly Princess must have felt as thankful as we do, that the days of such monstrosities have gone from England for ever, and that henceforth each can enjoy the liberty that is his inheritance. The Crown jewels came in for a large share of attention from the Princess, and seeing that in all probability they would one day be shared by

Her Royal Highness, the interest she displayed can be readily understood.

The Princess also paid her first visit to the Crystal Palace about this time, and spent some considerable time wandering about with the Prince without recognition from the public; only the two or three officials who were conducting them being aware of the rank of their distinguished visitors; at any rate for the first part of the day.

The day itself was rather a memorable one for the Palace, as for the first time the South-Eastern Railway Company had brought over a number of French excursionists for a day trip. Crowds of these had left Calais early that morning, and were enjoying themselves amazingly. The fine band of the "Sapeurs Pompiers" of St. Pierre had accompanied them, and these, getting to hear of the presence of the Prince and Princess, sought permission to play under the windows of the terrace rooms during dinner. This permission being accorded, they played a choice selection of music, finishing up with

"National Anthem," "Vive la Reine," and some ringing regular British cheers—a very gratifying proof of the universal popularity of our Queen and Royal family.

The following April, twenty thousand of

THE PRINCESS, 1866
WITH THE DUKE OF YORK AS A BABY
From a Photo. by W. & D. Downey

our citizen-soldiers were assembled at Brighton for a grand review; the town—always well filled—was on this occasion crowded to excess, as the Prince and Princess had signified their intention of being

present to view the proceedings. When their
Royal Highnesses appeared driving through
the streets towards the scene of action, the
weather was all that could be desired, and
the enthusiasm great; but unfortunately,
during the evolutions a terrific hail-storm
came on, which soon effectually cleared the
ground, and put an end to the programme.
Nevertheless, the visit had done good, inasmuch as it had stimulated our Volunteers, the
movement not being then so popular as it is
now; the War Office was not so ready with
its assistance, and the presence and interest
of the Prince and Princess would do much
to help what was then a very uphill cause.

Two or three other visits—each tending to
improve commerce generally—were paid just
about this time; one of which was to the
International Horticultural Exhibition, then
the best and largest ever known in England;
and another to the Horse Show at the Agricultural Hall, Islington.

In the month of June an event of great
interest occurred in the Royal family;

namely, the wedding of Her Royal Highness the Princess Mary of Cambridge. This Princess, as is well known, has the most striking presence of any one of the family: tall, handsome, majestic in the extreme, with so much native dignity and grace that she looks a veritable queen among women. Her Royal Highness has, too, one of the most amiable dispositions imaginable, and wins the steadfast affection and regard of every one with whom she comes in contact; with rich and poor alike she is a general favourite.

The wedding of this favourite Princess was quiet and simple in the extreme; she knew everybody in the vicinity of Kew, where she resided with her mother, the Duchess of Cambridge, and had a wish, as she said, to be "married among her own people." Accordingly, the marriage took place in the little parish church of Kew; and on the 12th of June, 1866, Princess Mary of Cambridge was united to Duke Francis of Teck. School-children strewed flowers, but

State ceremony was conspicuous by its absence; Her Majesty the Queen—cousin to the bride—together with the Prince and Princess of Wales, and many other members of the family, were present. The poor, also, were not forgotten, for, in addition to many of them being allowed to be present, they were afterwards feasted at the family's expense.

Less than a month had gone by and another Royal wedding was taking place; this time that of Princess Helena to Prince Christian, at Windsor Chapel. This must have brought back forcibly to the Princess of Wales the memory of her own marriage, it being celebrated at the same place, and in much the same manner, only of course upon a less expensive scale.

Perhaps of each of the Queen's daughters the Princess Christian is the best known in public. She has always resided in our midst, and always been ready to lend her valuable assistance to any deserving charitable cause, gracing not a few with her presence; and many philanthropic movements owe their success to the untiring zeal and devotion of Her Royal Highness the Princess Christian.

On the 7th of July in this year, the Princess of Wales performed the first public ceremony in her own name ; namely, the laying of the foundation stone of the Home for Little Boys at Farningham. To this, and to the continual interest Her Royal Highness has since displayed in this Institution, may be attributed much of the success which has ever characterised it. While the Princess is always willing to help a good and useful work, it may be noticed how much her sympathies always turn towards anything connected with children, and this cause indeed seems to call for special interest, when the otherwise friendless little ones are borne in mind. Many who would be quite destitute, and grow up devoid of care, to develop into criminals and outcasts, now find a good home and a useful education that fits them to take their place in the world as honest, and in some cases, prosperous men.

The Volunteers at Wimbledon again were honoured with the presence of the Prince and Princess, and those who were winners of principal prizes, deemed them of added value, as they had the privilege of receiving them from the hand of Her Royal Highness herself.

The Prince and Princess also visited York during the summer, where enormous preparations were made, and a right loyal reception accorded by our hospitable north countrymen.

The year 1867 was a rather clouded one for the Princess of Wales, as for several months she suffered much with rheumatism. It was during this illness, on the 20th of February, that the first daughter, Princess Louise, now Duchess of Fife, was born ; and for some considerable time much anxiety was felt on behalf of the Royal mother, the rheumatic complaint proving itself of a protracted nature. On the 18th of March, the Queen of Denmark came over to see her illustrious daughter, followed on the 20th by the King her father. All sorts of reports were prevalent owing to the visit of the King and Queen, but happily the illness had no serious results ; and although the recovery of Her Royal Highness was tedious, it was complete, except as regards a slight lameness, from which she has never thoroughly recovered. Of course all public engagements were cancelled, and all State and other duties had to be refused, so that a depression hung over society for some considerable period.

During the illness of the Princess, the suffering poor had not been forgotten, for on more than one occasion Her Royal Highness had caused presents of fruit and flowers to be sent to different hospitals for women and children.

In 1868 the Princess was again enabled to resume her active and useful life in our midst, to the sincere gratification of all classes of society. One of her first acts was to visit St. Bartholomew's Hospital, spending a considerable time in talking at the various bedsides of the sick and afflicted, cheering them with her gracious kindness and sympathetic manner.

The spring of this year was memorable for the first visit of Her Royal Highness to

THE PRINCESS, 1868
From a Photo. by Russell & Sons.

Ireland, accompanied, of course, by the Prince. The Princess on this occasion, in compliment to Ireland and in order to promote native industries, wore a dress of Irish poplin and a mantilla of Irish lace ; the Prince appearing in a green tie, and wearing shamrock in his buttonhole. The entire population turned out *en masse* to welcome the Royal couple, and every time they appeared in the streets during their visit, the utmost loyalty and heartiness of greeting was manifested. There was an utter absence of troops on every occasion,

entire confidence being placed in the good
faith and patriotic spirit of the people. A
very pretty ceremony, with a significant
meaning to it, took place at Kingston
Harbour, on the landing of the Prince and
Princess, and that was, a presentation to the
Princess, of a white dove as a token of
peace. And well was that peace preserved
during the entire stay among that much
traduced but warm-hearted people. Of all
that took place during that ten days' visit I
have not space to tell, but their Royal Highnesses must have really worked very hard,
so numerous were the various ceremonies
and entertainments in which they took part.

Of course the great event was the installation of the Prince as a Knight of St. Patrick,
in St. Patrick's Cathedral, Dublin. Her
Royal Highness the Princess was present,
and witnessed what, even to her, must have
been a very imposing ceremony.

Then there was a grand Review at
Phœnix Park, a State banquet given by the
Lord Lieutenant, a visit to the Cattle Show,

the Catholic University, Trinity College, the Hibernian University, two Hospitals, and a magnificent ball at the Exhibition Palace; and a visit of two or three days to Wicklow, where they had a better opportunity of viewing the fine scenery and becoming more closely acquainted with the manners and customs of the people. Only once do we find the Princess out on an expedition on her own account, and that was when she determined one afternoon to see the Alexandra College for ladies. Very much to the delight of the students, Her Royal Highness made herself familiar with the routine of duties, recreation, and accommodation, evincing the greatest interest in all she saw. This visit to Ireland was productive of much good feeling on the part of the Sister Isle, and gave general satisfaction to visitors and visited.

On the 6th of July, two days after Her Royal Highness had again visited the Crystal Palace, another daughter, the Princess Victoria, was born. And in the autumn, Glasgow was the scene of a Royal reception, when the Prince and Princess went to lay the foundation-stone of the new University building on Glasgow Hill.

CHAPTER VI

IN November the Prince and Princess went for a more extensive tour than any yet undertaken by them, first visiting the Emperor Napoleon at Compiégne, going from there to the Danish and Swedish Courts. Thus far on their journey their children had been with them, but as they intended being absent some time longer, they were now sent home, and the Prince and Princess proceeded to Berlin and Vienna, afterwards travelling to Alexandra and Cairo. At each place they were received with great rejoicing, every possible sort of entertainment being provided in their honour ; and here, as at home, all persons of all ranks were captivated by the charms of the Princess ; and the press of every country she visited continually sounded her praises. Hitherto, everything had been done on a scale of great magnificence, but, if splendour could surpass splendour, this was certainly the case during the latter part of their tour.

From Cairo the Prince and Princess with their suite proceeded up the Nile in a magnificent flotilla, then took up their abode for a season at the Palace of Kasr-el-Nil, amidst a scene of great pomp. Here every design that ingenuity and art could invent was produced; outside in the sand a beautiful garden was planted, and a flotilla of Nile boats was constantly in attendance under the Palace windows. They spent some five or six weeks in seeing the ruins of Luxor, Philæ and Karnac; and after returning to Cairo went on to the Pyramids of Girzeh, and so on from Alexandria to Constantinople.

They cast anchor at the "Golden Horn" in the first week in April, and after boarding the Sultan's State Caique, rowed to the Palace of Salek Bazaar, under the escort of

numerous Government Caiques. The Sultan
was there awaiting their arrival on the steps,
and having duly welcomed Their Royal
Highnesses, he conducted them to their
apartments. The residence here was the
height of Oriental luxury. Servants without
number stood in every direction, ready for
the slightest want. Such luxuries as pipes—
for ladies as well as gentlemen—and Turkish
baths were always on hand; every morning,
the Sultan sent presents of choice fruits and
flowers, every evening the finest musicians
in the country played during dinner; dinners,
by the way, composed in a wonderful and
fearful manner, as they generally consisted of
about twenty or twenty-four mixed dishes,
sweets and bitters, herbs and cucumbers
washed down with vinegar, &c. All the
habitués helped themselves with their fingers
in Oriental style.

Judging by records I have had the
pleasure of seeing—productions of one or
two members of the suite who accompanied
the Prince and Princess—the manners of

these palatial residents did not find very much favour with our English ladies. They were duly impressed with the unwonted splendour, but would, I think, have preferred a little less display, and a little more of our method of serving and eating. They could not manage the usual "pipe," and they certainly did *not* admire the ladies' dress, as they considered that the bunches worn round the legs, in divided skirts, or trousers fashion, "made them waddle like ducks."

Although the meals were not partaken of in our English method, they were served on gold and silver plate, and everything throughout was done in the same lavish style. Even the bedsteads at the disposal of the Prince and Princess were of solid silver, and were worth £3000 each. Carriages of costly build, and horses of rare breed awaited their pleasure; and a Guard of Honour was on duty, most magnificently equipped. Life there must have been like a dream, or the fairyland all of us firmly believed in as children.

The Prince and Princess, however, had one amusement apart from all this, and this was to steal away quietly alone, or with only one attendant, and go through the city in disguise, on foot, and plainly attired; passing as Mr. and Mrs. Williams.   They thus went to bazaars and shops, striking bargains here and there for anything that took their fancy, and partaking of the sweet and cooling beverages of the country, such as sherbet.

After a stay of about a fortnight, Their Royal Highnesses left, with many expressions of regret from the Sultan.   They then proceeded leisurely on their way, going first to visit the scenes of the Crimean War, and ultimately reaching home after an absence of about six months, the Princess now perfectly restored in health, and both of them in fact looking remarkably well.

Very soon after the return Her Royal Highness visited Earlswood Asylum.   This, as is generally known, is an Institution for idiots; children are admitted by vote, and all that is possible is done for the amelioration

of their sad condition. In accordance with
heir degrees of intelligence, they receive
general instruction and are taught various
trades. Nothing is perhaps more saddening
than to behold these of God's creatures, with
faces void of intellect, and often painfully
distorted, or quite repulsive; and many
would shrink from such an ordeal. This, in
fact, had diverted much charitable assistance
from this deserving cause; the directors
could not enlist the sympathies of the public
as they would have liked, as people would
not go and see for themselves; and, generally
speaking, when the object of charity is in
the background, the purse-strings are not so
loose.

When, therefore, the directors were aware
of the intended visit of Her Royal Highness,
they immediately meditated the usual con-
finement of the most afflicted inmates to a
part of the premises not on view. Of course
the motive was good, as they did not wish to
give the Princess any shock in viewing so
much that was painful. It seems, however,

that this reached the ears of Her Royal Highness, and she immediately caused a message to be conveyed that she "did not wish such a course ; she was interested in all whose suffering she tried to alleviate." Thus she set the noble example of subduing her own feelings to the requirements of others ; and not only Earlswood Asylum, but scores of other deserving charities have good cause to feel grateful to our Princess for her direct personal influence and practical help.

The most charming residence of the Prince and Princess of Wales is Sandringham House, near King's Lynn ; of this I shall have occasion to speak later ; but in July of this year (1869) I find them benefiting their local surroundings by going into King's Lynn to open the Alexandra Dock. A quiet sleepy little town is this King's Lynn, but it can wake up occasionally, and whenever it is favoured with the presence of its Royal neighbours, it is not a whit behind in manifestations of loyalty.

Manchester and Hull were also radiant

and patriotic that year, for both towns were gladdened by a brief stay of Their Royal Highnesses. The first-named place was filled to excess, as the Royal Agricultural Show was being held, and this event always attracts vast numbers from all parts ot England. Here a reception was afforded, brilliant and impressive; and giving abundant evidence of the popularity of the Royal couple.

In November, Princess Maud was born, the youngest daughter, and youngest surviving child of the Prince and Princess.

In March 1870, we find the Prince and Princess guests at Kimbolton Castle, the seat of the Duke of Newcastle. This is situated in the midst of some beautiful rural scenery, and a long country drive had to be taken from the nearest railway station, St. Neots. Several villages lay *en route*, and at each one resident families and cottagers all turned out in greeting.

In May, the new building for the University of London in Burlington Gardens was opened by Her Majesty the Queen, accompanied by the Prince and Princess of Wales.

On the 1st of July, Her Royal Highness is again assiduously performing her public duties, for on that day she accompanied the Prince to Reading, where His Royal Highness was to lay the foundation-stone of a new grammar school; this was chiefly a Masonic ceremony, and the order of Freemasons took part in the procession, and had the principal arrangements for the day. The inhabitants accorded themselves a general holiday, and Reading streets were rendered almost impassable by the enormous crowds surging to and fro. In addition to the decorations that had been liberally subscribed for, and were done in uniformity, nearly every householder had added to the display by flags and mottoes, and all the town was gay from end to end. Some hundreds of children occupied a stand in the London Road, with the intention of singing "God bless the Prince of Wales," as the Royal carriage passed; but, unfortunately, about half an hour prior to that event a part of the stand came down with a terrible crash! Every one was of course much alarmed, but the accident was not so serious as it might have been; one little lad was carried away to the hospital—which was close at hand—and it was reported that his leg was broken; but in a very short time— so great was his anxiety to see the Prince and Princess—he was brought back again in a bath-chair, and as the cheers at his reappearance were just dying away, a sound of music and cheering told that the Royal carriage was near. The first bars of the melody rose on the air, and then suddenly died away again; Her Royal Highness had noticed the gap in the stand, and with visible concern on her face, had the carriage stopped to inquire whether anything serious had occurred. The boy in the bath-chair was wheeled round to the front as the "only case," and had the honour of a few kindly words of commiseration. I was a small child then, and from where I stood I could view the whole proceeding.   How envious I felt of that boy, to be sure!   I never *had* had a broken leg, but I remember feeling I should not at all have minded having both my legs broken, if I could have gone to the Princess's carriage in a bath-chair.   When the procession moved on, the singing was again essayed, but it was of no use; there could be heard just about a dozen words, and then all the children broke out into shrill and deafening hurrahs.   I believe I shouted as loud as any of them, for if I could not get near the carriage, there was one thing I could do, and I did it too, quite to my own satisfaction.   I was, in common with nearly every man, woman and child, provided with flowers.   When the carriages were station-ary, I seized the opportunity, and with a confidence I should certainly lack now, I threw my flowers right into the carriage wherein their Royal Highnesses were sitting. I thought it a wonderful performance then, and was highly elated, yet at the same time a little bit afraid of the possible consequences; as although a small individual, I was old enough to understand that it was not polite to throw.

There was a grand ceremony in the tent where the stone was to be laid, and some excellent music by the Reading Philharmonic Society; afterwards followed by a luncheon in the Town Hall; then the Prince and Princess departed by special train, taking with them pleasant memories of their visit to the ancient town of Reading.

On the 7th of July, the Princess—together with three of her children—left England for a short sojourn in Denmark; the Prince escorting them as far as Calais. A longer stay was meditated in the first instance than was actually made; but, as will be within the memory of all, that year witnessed the outbreak of the Franco-German war, the declaration being made on the 19th of July. In consequence of this, the Princess and her children came home rather hurriedly.

The war continued to rage for some months; and partly owing to this, not many public engagements of note were entered into. The next of any importance was a visit to Edinburgh, the purpose being to lay the foundation-stone of the New Royal Infirmary; this was accomplished amidst much rejoicing, and many demonstrations of appreciation of the presence of the distinguished visitors.

A few days after this the Prince and Princess journeyed down to Chislehurst to visit the Empress Eugénie, who was then living in exile at Camden House; bereft of the companionship of her husband, and an alien from her country. This visit must have cheered and condoled the lonely and distressed lady in her solitude, and was an act of thoughtfulness on the part of the Prince and Princess which would be highly esteemed.

CHAPTER VII

In February 1871, Her Majesty the Queen opened Parliament in person, accompanied by Their Royal Highnesses the Prince and Princess of Wales. The "speech" on that occasion was unusually lengthy, and, among other things, announced the projected marriage of Her Royal Highness the Princess Louise to the Marquis of Lorne; which event was celebrated with much state at St. George's Chapel, Windsor, on the 21st of March. The Prince and Princess of Wales were present, the Princess looking as beautiful as ever; and her two boys, of whom she was evidently very proud, looking pretty and mischievous in Highland costume.

In April, the third son, and last child,

Prince Alexander, was born. His existence was of brief duration, for he died on the day succeeding his birth; and by his mother's desire was buried at Sandringham. The spot that marks his resting-place is in the little churchyard, on the side facing Sandringham House; the grave itself being of the plainest description. No costly and imposing marble monument, but just a little turf grave, surrounded with short gilt iron rails, and a headstone consisting of a white marble cross; "Alexander John Charles Albert, son of Albert Edward and Alexandra, Prince and Princess of Wales. 'Suffer little children to come unto Me.'"

For some little time after this the health of the Princess was anything but satisfactory, and the medical advisers ordered her to Kissingen and Schwalbach for the waters.

In the early winter the Prince and Princess honoured Lord Londesborough with a short stay at his place at Scarborough.

And now approaches an event which forms a history of itself :—the time of the illness of

His Royal Highness the Prince of Wales. On the 22nd of November, the report that he was stricken with typhoid fever was circulated throughout the length and breadth of the land, and the sympathy and concern of all classes was much aroused. On the 25th inst., the Queen went down to Sandringham to see her son, being of course, in the direst trouble at the terrible calamity. On Her Majesty's arrival, the children of the Prince and Princess, together with the children of the Princess Alice of Hesse—who was then on a visit to Sandringham—were sent off to Windsor; the Princess Alice herself staying to assist the Princess of Wales in nursing the sufferer.

The fever was apparently running its usual course, and with the best medical attendance of the day, and loving devoted nurses, there seemed no reason to expect other than a favourable issue; so on the 1st of December Her Majesty left Sandringham, hoping for the speedy recovery of her son.

For a few days His Royal Highness

G

was thought to be progressing; but quite
suddenly the most alarming symptoms set in,
and the gravest consequences were feared.
On the 8th inst., Her Majesty again hurriedly
journeyed to Sandringham, finding the Prince
unconscious and in the utmost danger.   The
entire country, nay, all the civilised world,
was filled with the deepest alarm, and
messages from all parts of the universe and
all shades and denominations of men, were
constantly arriving.   The illustrious patient
was the one theme of conversation in club,
drawing-room, office, and workshop; and as
the anniversary of the death of the lamented
Prince Consort drew near, a certain fore-
boding seemed to take hold of the people,
and the anxiety grew and intensified.   A
special prayer was offered in all the Churches,
at each service; and in every place of worship,
in India, States, and Colonies, in dissenting
churches and chapels, in Jewish synagogues,
and temples of Mohammedanism and Brah-
minism, the petition that the life of His
Royal Highness might be spared to his

family and to the people, was unceasingly made.

More than once, reports were circulated of his death, but the public were kept as well informed as was possible by the posting of bulletins in all prominent places. At length, just when the hopes of all were dying out, a slight improvement was noticed, and some hope of recovery entertained.

Only those who have had similar experiences, can form any idea of what this must have been to the anxious wife, mother, and sister, whose thoughts were all centred on the one so dear to them.

Perhaps one of the most touching incidents of the trying time was that of the Princess snatching a few minutes from the bedside of him she had so lovingly and so devotedly nursed and watched, in order that she might mingle her prayers with others of God's people in His own house. Knowing she could not stay through the entire service, Her Royal Highness sent a note to the Chaplain as follows :—

" My husband being, thank God, somewhat better, I am coming to Church. I must
leave, I fear, before the service is concluded,
that I may watch by his bedside. Can you
not say a few words in prayer in the early
part of the service, that I may join with you
in prayer for my husband before I return to
him ? "

The request was of course complied with,
and with faltering voice and perceptible
emotion the Rev. W. L. Onslow offered the
prayer, which was sincerely echoed in the
hearts of all present.

The improvement thus commenced went
steadily on, and soon all fear of a grave
termination to the illness was over. The
usual Christmas festivities were of necessity
dispensed with, but the gifts to the poor were
distributed in the presence of the Princess ;
General Knollys saying a few suitable words
to those assembled, assuring them of the
continued convalescence of the Prince ; and
thanking them for the sympathy they had
evinced. It would be difficult to say which

was uppermost with those assembled, cheers or tears.

On the 10th of February His Royal Highness was so far recovered as to be able to leave Sandringham for Windsor and Osborne, the Princess of course accompanying him, and indeed needing the change very much, as she was looking thin and pale, the result of her assiduous attention to her husband. They were so fortunate as to have a beautiful spring-like day for the journey, which was accomplished with very little fatigue. Although the time of starting and arriving was kept as quiet as possible, it leaked out here and there, and at some points little crowds of enthusiastically loyal people were assembled. Especially was this the case at Eton, where all the boys turned out and gave hearty cheers for the Prince and Princess.

Every English man and woman felt gratified at a message Her Majesty the Queen caused to be conveyed to the country at large, thanking them for their evident sympathy. The message concluded with these words :—" The Queen wished to express at the same time, on the part of the Princess of Wales, her feelings of heart-felt gratitude ; for she had been as deeply touched as the Queen, by the great and universal manifestation of loyalty and sympathy."

On the 27th of February a " National Thanksgiving " for the recovery of the Prince was celebrated in St. Paul's Cathedral, by a congregation consisting of thirteen thousand people ; composed of Her Majesty and the Royal Family, Members of the Government and Houses of Parliament, the Lord Mayor and Corporation, a large body of provincial Mayors, and a number of dis-tinguished personages of all professions. The streets presented the most enthusiastic display seen since the arrival of Her Royal Highness the Princess of Wales, in March 1863. Day by day as the time approached, the magnitude of the preparations had expanded.

The events of the progress through the

streets will be fresh in the minds of many of my readers ; the thirty thousand children in the Park, with their rendering of the " National Anthem," and their vociferous cheers ; the hearty plaudits of the tens of thousands of people gathered together ; the decorations, and all the features of a people's thanksgiving, cannot be forgotten by those who witnessed it.

When Her Majesty entered the Cathedral, the scene was most impressive ! The immense congregation—many of whom had been in their seats soon after 8 A.M.—rising to their feet at the first sound of the Royal trumpeters. The Queen, who was visibly affected, advanced, leaning on the arm of her beloved son, His Royal Highness the Prince of Wales, and leading one grandson by the hand ; the Princess of Wales walking on the left of Her Majesty leading another.

A slight deviation of route was made on the return journey, in order that the people might have a better opportunity of seeing the Royal family. Her Majesty, who looked smiling and happy, was dressed in black velvet and white ermine, and the Princess of Wales was in blue, with a black lace mantle. Every one was glad to see the Prince looking so far recovered as he did ; and fortunately the day was a very mild one, for the cheering was so continuous, that His Royal Highness carried his hat in his hand in response nearly the entire distance.

On reaching Buckingham Palace it would seem as though the people would never disperse ; cheer upon cheer rose on the air, and continued until the Queen, the Prince and Princess, came out on the balcony and bowed repeatedly in answer.

How much the mother, and the husband and wife, were moved and gratified by the events of the day may be gathered by yet another message to the people, as follows : " The Queen is anxious to express publicly her own personal very deep sense of the reception she and her dear children met with from millions of her subjects on her way to and from St. Paul's. Words are too weak for the Queen to say how very deeply touched and gratified she has been by the immense enthusiasm and affection exhibited towards her dear son and herself, from the highest down to the lowest, in the long progress through the capital, and she would most earnestly wish to convey her warmest and most heartfelt thanks to the whole Nation for this great demonstration of loyalty. The Queen, as well as her son and dear daughter-in-law, felt that the whole Nation joined with them in thanking God for sparing the beloved Prince of Wales's life. The remembrance of this day, and of the remarkable order maintained throughout, will for ever be affectionately cherished by the Queen and her family."

Change of air being prescribed, the Prince and Princess left England on the 9th of March for Paris and the South of France; they also visited Rome; and afterwards, joined by the Danish Royal family, went on to Florence, Venice, and Milan; taking the opportunity of inspecting several studios, and buying pictures and works of art ; then, having seen the Italian lakes, they turned their faces homewards.

Their Royal Highnesses were absent about three months, and travelled throughout as the Earl and Countess of Chester.

It was on the 1st of June 1872, that the Prince and Princess returned from their tour, just in the height of the London season. On the same afternoon they drove through Hyde Park, amidst one of the largest assemblies ever gathered there in expectation ; and were received with respectful salutations on all sides.

In the evening they attended the Royal Italian Opera, and on their entrance the entire house, together with the band, rose, and loudly cheered them.

On the 24th of June all the East End of London was on the tip-toe of expectation, for it was the day on which the Prince and Princess were to open the Bethnal Green Museum. The Royal visitors must have

been much amused at the quaint devices
that were displayed, such as : " Long wished-
for, come at last " ; " Welcome to the East " ;
" Come again, and bring your mother with
you " ; " Thank you for your kind visit," etc.
etc. If they were quaint though, they were
none the less loyal and affectionate ; and
many an East End son of toil shouted
himself hoarse in his greeting to the Prince
and his wife.

On the 11th of July the Princess performed
a work in aid of a cause in which she
was especially interested—the laying of the
foundation-stone of Great Ormond Street
Hospital for Children. This institute has
frequently since seen the Princess and
daughters within its walls, giving flowers,
fruit, toys, and, above all, loving words to
the little sufferers.

In the summer of 1873, the New Infirmary
at Wigan was opened by the Prince and
Princess, and on the following day, the
ceremony of opening the Town Hall at
Bolton was performed. Vast crowds were

assembled on each day, and the entire towns
were jubilant, a general holiday being
observed.

On the 16th of June, the Grand Duchess
Czarevna, now Empress Mother of Russia,
and sister of the Princess of Wales, came
over on a visit, much to the delight of Her
Royal Highness. No doubt the two sisters
would have many confidential little chats
about old times, and about their present
experiences in the respective Courts in which
they each shone as leading stars.

The same month saw the visit of the Shah
of Persia, and all London society was given
over to entertaining and lionising His
Majesty. Of course the Prince and Princess
of Wales had to take a very prominent part in
the entertaining ; not the least of which was
a dinner party at Marlborough House. My
readers will readily understand that the Shah
of the first visit was not the Shah of a sub-
sequent visit ; and not quite so conformable
to English customs.

CHAPTER VIII.

On January 10th in the following year, the Prince and Princess left England for St. Petersburg, in order to be present at the marriage of His Royal Highness the Duke of Edinburgh to Her Imperial Highness the Grand Duchess Marie, only daughter of Alexander II. of Russia. The wedding festivities were conducted in a superb manner; and many and various were the entertainments provided for the Royal visitors, one of which was a grand parade of troops.

During that summer their Royal Highnesses first used the new yacht Osborne; which has so often since been their floating home off the Isle of Wight.

In the latter part of July, a fancy ball—

almost the first—was given by the Prince and Princess at Marlborough House, trades and industries being largely represented.   In November, a visit was paid to Birmingham, and strong interest was shown in the various manu-factories.

On the 6th of the follow-ing April, the Prince and Princess took part in the Installation ceremony con-nected with the transfer of the Merchant Taylors' school to the Charterhouse, much to the delight of the boys of those schools. This year was the date of Messrs. Moody and Sankey's mis-sion services, which were

THE PRINCESS, 1874
From a Photo. by Russell & S⟨

generally well patronised. One of the places in which they held their services was the Haymarket Theatre ; and here, one after-noon in April, Her Royal Highness the Princess of Wales quietly entered ; and

took a seat to listen to the famous evan-
gelists.

On the 18th of April, their Royal Highnesses were
present at the
"restoration"
services at
St. Margaret's,
King's Lynn;
which restora-
tion had been
carried out
at a cost of
£60,000, as a
memorial of
the happy re-
covery of the
Prince from his
serious illness.

THE PRINCESS, 1874
From a Photo. by Russell & Sons.

The entire
County turned out to welcome their honoured
and beloved neighbours.

Early in May, Her Majesty the Queen
gave a party to all her grandchildren, by this

time growing numerous.   Not the quietest of
this merry Windsor gathering were the two
boys of the Prince and Princess of Wales ;
who were pretty generally on mischief bent

wherever they
were, and a
sort of mixed
blessing to
elderly rela-
tions.

In October
of that year,
the Prince
started on his
Indian visit,
the Princess
on this occa-
sion going
with her hus-
band as far as

THE PRINCESS, 1876
From a Photo. by Russell & Sons.

Calais.   His Royal Highness was absent
for seven months, and during that time
his life was one continual journeying
to and fro ; from one festival to another

that loyal India had convened in his honour.

On his return on the 11th of May, 1876, he had an im-posing greet-ing from all classes. The Channel was literally alive with steamers crowded with passengers anxious for a first glimpse.

The Prin-cess and the children were there on board the

THE PRINCESS, 1876

From a Photo. by Russell & Sons.

Enchantress, the landing taking place at Portsmouth.

On the 14th the entire family went to Westminster Abbey to a Thanksgiving Service for the safe return of His Royal

H

Highness; and on the 17th the Prince and Princess attended in state a congratulatory concert at the Royal Albert Hall.

In October their Royal Highnesses laid the foundation-stone of the new Post Office at Glasgow; and this time their two boys were of the party; they enjoyed their visit thoroughly, and the Scotsmen were delighted to see them in their midst.

THE PRINCESS, 1876
From a Photo. by Russell & Sons

On the 26th of November the Prince and Princess visited Norwich in support of a movement in aid of a local hospital. Their Royal Highnesses have done much to help charities in the neighbourhood of their Norfolk residence ; and the kindly help has placed several of these local institutes on a sound financial basis.

In March 1877, Charing Cross Hospital welcomed their Royal Highnesses to the ceremony of opening a new wing just completed. One ward, intended for children, was, by permission of the Princess, named the Alexandra Ward. At the close of the formal proceedings, Her Royal Highness made a tour of the various wards, conversing with many of the patients.

In April a pleasant Continental trip was taken by the Royal couple, in order to visit the King and Queen of Greece ; and a little later in the year, an impressive ceremony took place at Wantage, when the statue of Alfred the Great was unveiled by the Prince, in the presence of a large and distinguished assembly ; her Royal Highness the Princess also being present, and, as usual, being the centre of attraction.

This same year, the Princes Albert Victor

and George were placed on board the
Britannia at Portsmouth as cadets, their
parents wisely determining to have an early
and practical training imparted to their boys;
and here be it said, that the young cadets
were treated exactly the same as all the
others on board, the same duties had to be
performed, and the same regulations were
enforced. There is no doubt this training
did much to impart the manly and resolute
character to the young Princes which afterwards distinguished them. ·

Unfortunately the entrance of Prince
Albert Victor for training was somewhat
delayed on account of an attack of typhoid
fever, so his brother had time to make
acquaintance with his new friends, and to
fully establish his identity—a process which
did not take that young gentleman long to
accomplish, for he was soon known as an
undoubted leader in mischief of every description, and was voted "no end of a
brick." At the same time he was assiduous
in his duties, and quickly became thoroughly

conversant with the technicalities of his profession.

In 1878 several important visits were paid by the Prince and Princess ; but perhaps the one that the Princess felt most interest in was the visit to the cadet ship at Dartmouth, a place which held part of her world, so to speak. Everybody knows what a mother Her Royal Highness is, and everybody would understand how proud she would feel of her boys, when, on the occasion of the visit of the Prince and herself, they were in the boat to take them alongside—one to steer and the other to pull in the crew. I do not suppose their father's pride was so manifest—men never do show their exultation much—but it was there all the same, for the Prince of Wales is a devoted parent, and very fond and proud of his children. The occasion of the visit to the cadet ship was to distribute the medals and prizes to the fortunate recipients, and a very interesting time they had with these sturdy young English sailors.

One grand work on the part of their Royal Highnesses was their visit to Brompton, in order to lay the foundation-stone of the new Hospital for Consumption, that most fatal of English diseases.

Greenwich was also honoured this year, the Prince and Princess, the two young Princes, and the Duke of Cambridge going down to give the prizes to the boys at the Royal schools. Various exercises were gone through by the boys, short speeches were spoken, and large cheers given for visitors, prize-takers, and everything and everybody that the boys could shout for ; but perhaps as worthy of note as anything that happened during the day, was an act of kindness rendered by the Princess of Wales. It appears that the wife of the Superintendent was lying ill, and to her great disappointment could not be present. Hearing of this, Her Royal Highness quietly slipped away and, going to the invalid's room, sat chatting with her for some considerable time.

In July the Midland Counties Art Museum

was opened at Nottingham by Their Royal Highnesses, in the presence of an immense concourse of people.

In the following year the Convalescent Home at Hunstanton was opened by the Prince and Princess. The funds at the disposal of the Committee had not yet permitted of more than the actual building and fitting, and subscribers were sadly needed in order that the forty beds might be turned to practical account, for the benefit of those for whom they were intended. With true kindness, the Princess came forward to the aid of the Committee, and promised herself to support one bed! Such a generous example could not fail of imitation! Immediately the entire number were subscribed for, and the Home had an auspicious beginning.

Another cause that the Princess specially interested herself in at this time was the Chelsea Hospital for Women. Her Royal Highness not only laid the stone for the building, but also attended an old English fancy fair at the Albert Hall on its behalf.

The funds which were realised at the Hall, and the amount in purses received by the Princess at the laying of the stone, resulted

THE PRINCESS, 1879
From a Photo. by Russell & Sons

in a grand total of £7000. Many hundreds of poor women have had cause to bless the name of the noble woman, who, feeling for the sufferings of others, came forward to assist in their alleviation.

Another pleasant visit was paid to Denmark, such visits being more and more prized by the King and Queen, now that their home circle had gradually grown so much smaller.

During the next year Her Royal Highness had the pleasure of a visit from her brother the King of the Hellenes ; and among other festivities taking place in his honour, may be mentioned a civic event, namely, the conferring of the freedom of the City of London on His Majesty, the Prince and Princess being present on the occasion.

In July Their Royal Highnesses opened the last five of the Thames bridges free to the public, the toll being taken off for ever ; this had been much wished for by all business people, the payment for use of those bridges having been irksome to them in the extreme. It was also a great boon to thousands of the working classes, who had to cross in order to get to their various avocations.

The Prince and Princess also visited Portsmouth, and with Her Majesty the Queen went over the troopship *Jumna*, then lying alongside.

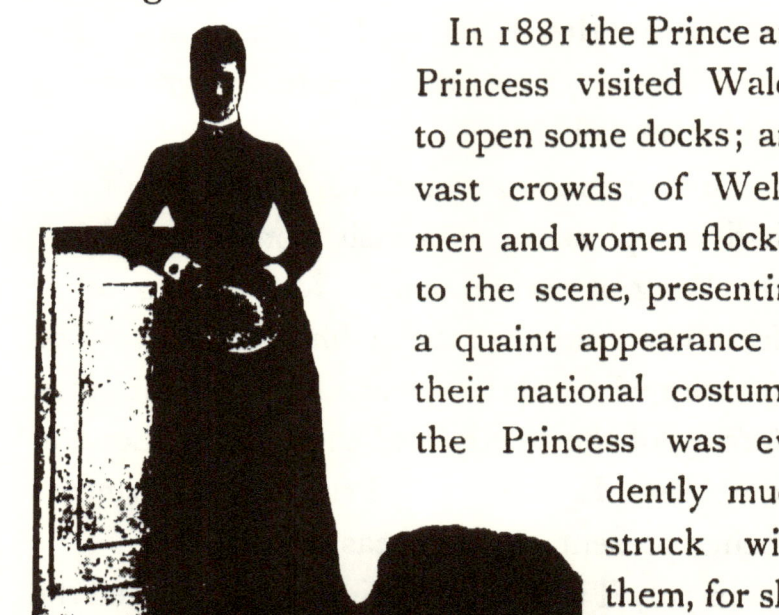

THE PRINCESS, 1880

From a Photo. by Russell & Sons

In 1881 the Prince and Princess visited Wales, to open some docks; and vast crowds of Welsh men and women flocked to the scene, presenting a quaint appearance in their national costume; the Princess was evidently much struck with them, for she called two of the country girls with rosy faces and sugar-loaf hats to her side, and asked them many questions, to their great trepidation, yet delight, and to the envy of all the other girls around. One feature of the proceedings was the singing of the " Men of Harlech " by a choir of two thousand voices.

Another event is worthy of record, showing the kind thoughtfulness of the Princess for

THE PRINCESS, 1880
From a Photo. by Russell & Sons

the very poorest of the land, and that is the visit of Her Royal Highness to the Marylebone Workhouse, when she walked round, and talked pleasantly with numbers of the inmates.

A National Fisheries Exhibition was opened this year at Norwich by the Prince and Princess, and proved to be a very successful undertaking. So much so, that the Prince then first formed the idea for the London yearly exhibitions that became such a feature.

CHAPTER IX

In 1882 all England was aroused by the terrible murders of Lord Frederick Cavendish and Mr. Burke, soon after their arrival in Dublin to take up the duties of the respective appointments they had just received. It was on Saturday, the 6th of May, that these two gentlemen were shot in Phœnix Park, as they were proceeding together across it on foot. The indignation of the English was unbounded, and the greatest commiseration was felt and expressed for the families of the two unfortunate victims. The Prince and Princess hastened to call on Lady Frederick Cavendish, the Princess, with womanly sympathy, endeavouring to comfort the bereaved widow. At no period of modern history has such a dastardly deed been committed in open day-

light, and within musket-shot of soldiers of
an all-powerful country. This was truly an
act that will for ever leave a stain of the
blackest hue on those who were the instigators
of the foul crime, and on the land in which it
was committed. Probably by no one was
the deed more deplored than by all loyal
Irishmen.

On the 20th of May, the Prince and Princess went down to Truro, in order to lay the
foundation-stone of the Cathedral. Needless
to say, it was the scene of a grand episcopal
ceremony, the civic authorities of course
taking part in the function; the place was
beautifully decorated, and the event a note-
worthy one in every respect.

In the autumn, the two boys of the Prince
and Princess came home from their first trip
in the *Bacchante*; and great was the family
rejoicing at the meeting. Merry times the
young people must have had in their favourite
Sandringham home, and very much to tell
each other of all that had transpired since
their separation; although it can easily be

imagined that the sisters' accounts of visits
paid and received, arrival of new pet animals,

WHIPPINGHAM CHURCH
From a Photo.

and deaths of cherished ones, particulars of
children in Royal schools, and protégés in
model cottages, would all fade into insignifi-

cance beside the brothers' tales of life and of
adventures in foreign climes.

Soon after their return, the two Princes
were confirmed, the solemn ceremony taking
place at Whippingham Church, in presence
of Her Majesty the Queen, the Prince and
Princess, and a large number of the Royal
Family. Very earnest would be the prayers
of their God-fearing mother for her boys, on
this, the first public promise made by them
for their future lives.

1883 witnessed the opening of the Royal
College of Music, an institution that owes its
origin to the Prince and Princess of Wales.
The college supplies a long-felt want, and
provides a sound musical education for a
smaller outlay than the old time-honoured
academies and schools.

In May, the longed talked of " Fisheries "
was opened, and proved itself an enormous
success, exceeding the most sanguine expec-
tations. Here, again, was a great National
work brought about by the Prince and his
accomplished wife, and all England was

benefited by the large amount of interest and the great influx of visitors it attracted.

On one occasion deputations of fishermen and fisher-girls were brought up to London, and all appeared in the costume of their calling at the Exhibition ; all enjoying the, to them, unaccustomed sight, and the wonders that met them at every turn. But a greater treat was in store for them the next day, for the Prince and Princess graciously invited them all to Marlborough House, and there talked to them on the lawn, afterwards causing them to be entertained in the servant's hall. I have no doubt that these fisher-folk still continue to tell admiring auditors of "the day when they went to the Prince's house up in London, and how the lovely Princess came and talked to them." Better than a fairy tale this will be to the little ones because it is all true, and "father and mother were there."

More was to come, however, for then the Baroness Burdett-Coutts had a treat in store for them ; and if I keep you waiting one

minute before I tell you what it was, it is
that I may here pay a tribute of esteem to
her ladyship on behalf of my fellow country-
women. Wherever the name of the Baroness
is heard—and it is heard on every hand—
it is honoured, and rightly too; for surely
few women have done for the poor of the
land what she has done. Her ear has been
ever open to the tales of want and misery
which so unfortunately abound, and she has
been ever ready to assist with material and
substantial help all who have deserved such
assistance. Of her it may be truly said,
" She hath done what she could."

This universal friend to the poor came
forward on this occasion to promote the
enjoyment of these hard-working fisher-folk,
and when they had finished their repast at
Marlborough House she had them all conveyed in carriages to the Zoological Gardens,
where they spent some considerable time
in admiring the inhabitants of the various
houses and cages. Afterwards, they were
all taken to her ladyship's house in Picca-

dilly, and there regaled with a substantial repast.

One great result of this Exhibition was the interest aroused on behalf of these sons of toil who get their living on the briny wave, and endure hardships of which we have no conception, endangering their lives in order to minister to our wants.

I am glad to say these people have a warm and substantial friend in the Baroness, and much has been done to mitigate their sufferings and alleviate their wants.

In August the Princess and her daughters made a short stay in Devonshire. During this stay, an incident occurred a little out of the common. When bouquets are presented it is generally from the hands of ladies or children that the Princess receives them, but on this occasion an old fisherman, who had saved no less than twenty lives, and had, moreover, fought at Navarino, was the one who offered a large bunch of flowers for the acceptance of the Princess. Needless to say the flowers were accepted with as sweet a smile as any gift ever offered to Her Royal Highness, and with a few words of gracious commendation of the noble deeds of the brave old warrior and fisherman.

In 1884 a Forestry Exhibition was held in Edinburgh, the Prince and Princess being present to perform the opening ceremony.

Their Royal Highnesses also paid a visit to Worcester, when they visited several porcelain factories, viewed the various processes of manufacture in which they were much interested, and made some considerable purchases.

In September the Prince and Princess went to Newcastle to open a public park, the gift of Lord Armstrong to the town. The interest of the occasion was still further enhanced by the planting of a tree by Her Royal Highness the Princess.

Now approaches a year fraught with unusual interest to the royal lady of whom I am writing, and to her husband and children; and that is, the coming of age of the eldest son, Prince Albert Victor. The years had

·indeed sped on since Alexandra, Princess of Denmark, made her triumphant entry into England, and won her place in the hearts of English people. Now her firstborn had arrived at the age and dignity of manhood, and all the neighbourhood of Sandringham was *en fête* to welcome the auspicious day, the 8th of January, 1885. Great numbers of presents flowed in from all directions : private presents from Her Majesty down to the one from the servants ; and Municipal offerings conveyed by various deputations with the ever-present addresses.

All the labourers on the estate—numbering between two and three hundred—proceeded to the house to cheer and congratulate the Prince ; while the school children, from their places in the avenue, added their shrill voices to the chorus ; every child being duly regaled with wonderful packets of good things from the well-filled baskets that were carried round.

Very soon a procession came into view, which was a veritable wonder to all the rustic beholders, the majority of whom had never journeyed far from their native village. Sanger's Circus, with all its glitter of silver and gold, all its gay colouring, its prancing steeds bearing men in armour and beautiful ladies, appeared through the Norwich gates and proceeded up the avenue. Such a collection of wonder-struck faces had surely never assembled beneath those trees before, and when everybody was let into the large tent, specially erected, free of charge, the admiration was unbounded, and only found vent in repeated and vociferous applause.

Then there was a dinner for all the men, and a tea for women and children, to which you may be quite sure ample justice was done. After that came the illumination of the park by Pain and Sons; the many thousands of coloured lamps lighting up avenues, gardens, and lakes, presenting a spectacle of much grandeur and picturesqueness.

To close the day's proceedings, a grand ball was given, to which over one thousand guests were invited. The appearance of the ball-room was indescribably grand ; the glitter of light arms and trophies on the walls, the floral decorations, the magnificent dresses and jewellery and the brilliant uniforms, made up a picture of striking beauty, the strains of music adding to the effect. On this occasion, the Prince, whose natal day was being celebrated, led his mother down the room when the Royal Family entered in couples, Her Royal Highness looking surpassingly beautiful and radiantly happy.

Various high honours were conferred upon the young Prince, including English and Foreign Orders ; he was also made a Bencher of the Middle Temple and a Freemason.

Another hospital was opened that year by the Prince and Princess, namely, the " Royal National," situated in Queen Square, for sufferers from paralysis and epilepsy.

In April the Prince and Princess, accompanied by Prince Albert Victor, went to Ireland, and took part in a number of functions organised in their honour. The first

was to lay the foundation-stone of the new
Science and Art Museum and National
Library of Ireland; an Institution calculated to
do much for the young Ireland of the future.

The degree of Doctor of Laws was conferred on
Prince Albert
Victor, and
that of Doctor
of Music on
the Princess
of Wales. We
are all familiar
with the char-
ming picture
of Her Royal
Highness in
her trencher

THE PRINCESS IN DOCTOR'S ROBES, 1885
From a Photo. by Lafayette, Dublin

and robes; and certainly from a musical
point of view, the robe rests on one who
is fully qualified for the honour, the Princess being a musician of a very high order.
A tour of eight or nine days to view some
of the far-famed scenery was taken by

the Royal visitors, who then returned to Dublin.

An interesting event was the presentation of an address by ten thousand Protestant Sunday School children, these being formed up in order outside the Vice-Regal Lodge.

Belfast was honoured with a visit, and from there the Royal party

ENGLISH CHURCH, COPENHAGEN
From a Photo. by Gunn & Stuart.

returned to London, after an absence of three weeks in the sister Isle.

In the summer Princess Louise, the eldest

daughter, " came out " ; and in the last week of July, all three of the daughters of the Princess of Wales were bridesmaids to their aunt, Her Royal Highness the Princess Beatrice

In the autumn the entire family proceeded to Denmark ; and the Princess was then able to initiate the carrying out of a long cherished scheme, by laying the foundation-stone of an English Church at Copenhagen.

A pleasant Hungarian trip was then taken, enabling the Princess to be present at the wedding of her youngest brother.

In 1886 the Prince and Princess opened the new bridge between Fulham and Putney, which had been built at a cost of £240,000, and is certainly one of the handsomest of the bridges of which Londoners are so justly proud.

In June they again visited the East End of London ; this time to lay the foundation-stone of the Queen's Hall, one of the adjuncts of the People's Palace. The greetings of the toilers were hearty and enthusiastic, and were doubtless accepted in the spirit in which they were offered.

In the same month their Royal Highnesses opened a new wing to the Royal Victoria Hospital, Chelsea, thus helping another of the many similar institutions with their influential presence.

In the early autumn the Princess of Wales had an attack of diphtheria; and needing a change, Torquay was the place selected. Her Royal Highness and daughters made some considerable stay here, visiting most places of note in the neighbourhood, and spending most of their

THE PRINCESS, 1886
From a Photo. by Russell & Sons.

time in exploring amongst the rich and picturesque scenery with which the place abounds. A very pretty little ceremony, performed by the fishermen of Torquay and the adjacent places, took place one morning in honour of Her Royal Highness. About fifty of the " smacks " formed up into squadron, and " dipped flags." Having done this opposite to where Her Royal Highness was staying, they then proceeded on their way to their daily work, satisfied that they had paid the honour, though too far off to see how it was received; but feeling, doubtless, the same confidence as all do, in the appreciation by the Princess of the loyalty and respectful affection intended.

The next year, 1887, was an important year in the history of this country, being the Jubilee of Her Most Gracious Majesty, Queen Victoria. Literally, from all parts of the world, kings, princes, and men of note came hither to pay their respectful congratulations to the wisest and best Queen that ever filled the throne of England.

To speak of the various celebrations and festivities that took place in that eventful year would fill a book in itself. Of course the Prince and Princess of Wales were, next to the Queen, the centre of attraction in the different ceremonies ; but I must content myself with noting events, more particularly appertaining to their own family, or to visits in aid of charities made by themselves alone.

That year witnessed the " coming out " of the Princess Victoria, the second daughter, and the joining of the 19th Lancers by Prince Albert Victor ; this event taking place soon after His Royal Highness had, in the presence of the Prince and Princess, taken his degree at Cambridge.

In May the Prince and Princess, accompanied by the Crown Prince of Denmark, visited the London Hospital, to open a nursing home, college, library, &c. The Royal party went through the wards, speaking to several of the sufferers ; and the Princess, with her usual and well-known sympathy and interest for children, took her bouquet to pieces, and distributed the flowers until there was not one left.

A visit was also paid by the Princess and

her daughters to Tottenham, where they opened a small wing to the Deaconesses' Institute and Hospital.

The Prince, Princess and daughters, made yet another journey to Mile End, this time to be present at the opening of the People's Palace ; a place of recreation that was sorely needed, and is much appreciated by the working classes.

Another, and a most interesting charitable work I must not omit to record, and that is a concert, given by the Princess and her daughters, to the patients and nurses of the Brompton Hospital ! The Royal ladies played several duets, trios, and quartets, the Princess also taking pianoforte in a duet for that instrument and the violin, as well as playing the accompaniments of several songs. Here is an example that might well be followed by numbers who have no other occupation than " killing time," and whose education and abilities fit them for the like task, did they choose to take the trouble to cheer and amuse their less fortunate fellow creatures.   After the concert, the ladies made a tour of the wards, and then partook of tea previous to their departure.

Just about this time I was present at an event in the North of London, which the Princess and daughters had graced with their presence ; and had had to make a journey from Norfolk in order to do so.   As there had been so much uncertainty as to the visit, very little preparation had been made ; and as a result, the crowd had it almost their own way.   The manner in which the Royal ladies were hustled was surely "an uncommon and particular event," but they very evidently much enjoyed the fun!   Just before they left, a few flowers, hastily captured, and done into veritable dress sprays, were presented by a child of six, and were as graciously accepted as though the offering were the choicest bouquet proffered with rehearsed effect.

Another of the cherished schemes of Her Royal Highness was about this time carried into effect : as long as three years before she had suggested it, and now saw the fruition of her plans.   I refer to the opening of Alexandra House, at Kensington.   This is a home for women students in different schools of art, music, and science.   There are between fifty and sixty suites of rooms, each suite consisting of two bed-rooms and a sitting-room to be shared between two students.   There is also a suite of practising rooms for music, and a suite of art studios ; a gymnasium, and a large concert-hall ; and in addition a fine drawing-room, with good library, dining-room of noble proportions, and other necessary offices.

Another visit was paid to Denmark in the autumn, and this time the family gathering was unusually large, being increased by the Emperor and Empress of Russia and family. The English church before mentioned was by this time finished, and was consecrated during the visit of the various members of the Danish family to the city.   The stay at the Summer Palace of Bernstorff was more protracted than was intended in the first instance ; as, unfortunately, measles broke out in the Palace, and all the youthful visitors had it. However, they each recovered in due time, and returned none the worse for their temporary affliction.

CHAPTER X

THE year 1888 was a very shadowed year for the English Court and Royal Family, on account of the deaths of the two German Emperors. The silver wedding of the Prince and Princess—which would have been under ordinary circumstances the occasion for a national display of loyalty—passed over in a very quiet manner. Presents and testimonials of regard and esteem were numerous, but no public rejoicings were indulged in; and Their Royal Highnesses merely gave a family dinner-party to celebrate the event, Her Majesty the Queen coming up from Windsor in order to be present. I shall not attempt a description of the presents, but mention only one or two: one—a gift that was highly valued by Her Royal Highness—

was from her children, and took the form of a silver model of her favourite mare "Vera." They also, for the same occasion, made the Prince a present of a similar model of his favourite hunter. The members of the West Norfolk Hunt, with whom the Prince has hunted for over thirty years, presented him with a silver model of a fox. Speaking of the silver wedding, reminds me that this is the first time that a Prince of Wales has celebrated such an event.

THE PRINCESS, 1888
From a Photo. by Russell & Sons

In May the Prince and Princess opened the Anglo-Danish Exhibition in London; and in the same month went to Glasgow to open an Exhibition there: they were the guests of Lord Hamilton at Dalzell. On their way home, they stopped at Blackpool to lay

the foundation-stone of the Technical
School.

On the 15th of June the Prince and Princess,
accompanied by their daughters, unveiled
the statue of Sir Bartle Frere, on the Thames
Embankment; and on the 15th of July—
in fulfilment of a long-standing promise—
Their Royal Highnesses opened the Great
Northern Hospital at Holloway.

In 1889 Her Majesty the Queen paid a
visit to her son's Sandringham home; and
as this was the first time since the dangerous
illness of the Prince, when the two visits
were strictly private, an account of the three
or four days spent there may be of some
interest.

" Is it true the Queen of all England be
a-coming t'here ? " " Yes." " Then we shall
ha' main foine toimes." " Ha' yer ever seen
her ? " " What be she loike ? " Such and
similar questions were propounded on every
hand by the villagers.

As a rule, Royalty come and go at Sandringham and very little notice is taken, so

much are the people accustomed to their
presence in their midst. Now, however,
there really was something worth turning out
for, and speculation was rife in hall and
cottage; and as soon as the announcement
was confirmed, preparations were extensively
made on every hand. At last the eventful
day arrived, and half Norfolk was on the
qui vive; but, sad to relate, instead of the
well-known Queen's weather, the skies wore
a leaden hue, and the rain came down steadily,
and continued to do so until just before Her
Majesty arrived about 6 P.M. Very gay and
beautiful the avenues would have looked
under different circumstances; nevertheless
the people were there. *They* were not to be
cheated out of the sight which they might
never again have the opportunity of gazing
upon; so there they waited, in all their best
clothes, bravely donned for the occasion—
afoot and horseback, landau, waggonette,
and village cart. The popular Comptroller,
Sir Dighton Probyn, was busy galloping
backwards and forwards to see that every-

thing and everybody was in the appointed place.

The first sight was the Prince and his

THE DUKE OF CLARENCE
From a Photo. by W. & H. Downey

eldest son going down to the station on their way to King's Lynn to meet Her Majesty. However, we Norfolkites can see them every

day, and so very little notice is taken.
Shortly after the Princess and daughters
drive down to Wolferton Station. This is
a little better, for feminine curiosity is aroused
as to what they "have got on." Much
patient waiting ensues, and imagination pictures the scene at Lynn Station, where the
Queen is to receive addresses, bouquets, &c.
Now at last the train steams into Wolferton,
and Her Majesty alights ; and after greeting
the Princesses, and having one or two pre-
sentations made her, she proceeds to the
handsome waiting-rooms, built by the Prince
in 1875. In one or two minutes the procession moves out into the avenue. Scarlet
coats lead the way, but not the military
scarlet. We have here a novel escort for
Her Majesty, in the shape of the West
Norfolk Hunt. About sixty or seventy of
these splendidly mounted gentlemen lead the
way.

The Royal carriages follow, and as the
Queen's is an open one, every one has a good
view. Very well and very happy she looks,

too ; with her son's wife at her side, and her
son and grandson riding on either hand.
Cheer upon cheer rises on the evening air—
Norfolk people *can* shout. Everything on
wheels, and everybody mounted, and as
many pedestrians as could keep up, followed
in the rear. And it was an eager, excited,
and loyal crowd that reached the entrance
almost as soon as Her Majesty did.

Here a pretty sight bursts upon them, for
inside the gates are the school children in
their bright red cloaks, the keepers in their
livery of tan and green, and the gentlemen
of the hunt, who have ridden quickly in and
taken up their position in the rear on either
side. There is the band and guard of
honour of the Norfolk Militia, the triumphal
arch, and other decorations—all contributing
to make up a picture not easily forgotten by
those who witnessed it.

Then the Queen and family alight, and
make their way to the entrance saloon ; and
immediately another interesting ceremony
takes place. The huntsmen once more move

forward, not to "Tally-ho," but with more dignified mien. The Queen appears at an open window, and every gentleman, with hat in hand, rides slowly by in single file. The movement, though slow, is not silent, for every huntsman cheers to the echo, all faces looking well pleased with the Royal smiles beaming upon them.

Sandringham has quite an army of servants, but the preparations were of necessity very extensive, and the scrubbing and rubbing, arranging and re-arranging that has gone on for a week or more before this visit has been wonderful. Now everything is done ; *chefs* have done their utmost, dinner is served, and a right joyous family party sit down to partake of it.

That dinner, however, is not the only one that has had to be prepared, for a marquee has been specially erected, and all the tenants and labourers have been made happy by printed invitations from the Comptroller, desiring their presence at dinner in aforesaid marquee. Some of these invitations are now

proudly exhibited in the homes of the
tenantry, framed and hung in prominent
places ; they, together with jubilee cups and
saucers (two of which were given to every
tenant and labourer), are highly prized.

To return to the feasting : not only are the
adults provided for, but the children have a
tea ; and the day, begun under rather miser-
able auspices, ends with rejoicing.

Next morning Her Majesty is about in
good time, as usual ; and, breakfast having
been served in her own apartments, she
goes round on a tour of inspection, not-
withstanding the falling rain.

First the church is visited, then the rectory, and after that the school children are
made happy by seeing the Queen inspect
their domain.

After luncheon it clears up a little, and out
they all go again.

This time the Queen and Prince in an
open carriage, all the others—Princess of
Wales, her son and daughters, and the
Princess Louise of Lorne—in a waggonette.

This is a favourite mode of locomotion with the family, and very jolly and happy they look, all packed in together.

First they drive off to Castle Rising, not to inspect the home which was shortly to have for its mistress the Princess Louise of Wales, but merely to see the ruin of the old Castle, first founded in 1176. It is worth a visit, and evidently the Queen thinks so.

However, they do not linger here. Her Majesty has come to Sandringham to see what there is to be seen, and as she is only to pay a three days' visit things must be got over quickly. The Prince has a nice dairy farm he wants his mother to see, so in this direction they drive.

The Queen also has a dairy farm, and much discussion and nodding and shaking of heads ensues over the various methods employed, &c.

Then there are some fine breeds of sheep to inspect, and a number of horses the Prince has been investing in : all these pass muster ; then the Princess has her turn. She has her

dairy, aye, and knows how to work it too ; for
Her Royal Highness and her daughters are
quite capable of making butter, and often do
so.   There is not time now to let the Queen
see *how* capable these Royal ladies are of
performing dairy work, but there *is* time for
a quiet, comfortable cup of tea, such as the
Royal soul loveth, and there is such a
charming tea-room that joins the Princess's
dairy, it would be a pity not to rest there, it
looks so inviting ; so a general seating ensues,
and the cup that cheers, &c., goes gaily
round, and then everybody goes home to
dress.

There is a remarkable absence of sight-
seers. Certainly every one would have to come
a considerable distance to see the Queen, but
then she has not given them the opportunity
for about seventeen years, so one would
almost expect them.   Even " our special cor-
respondent " is conspicuous by his absence.
Poor deluded souls, after trying to find out
where Her Majesty intended going that day,
they all went off to just where she did *not* go,

and there they patiently waited until it got too late to expect her, then went home disconsolate.

This sort of thing continued throughout the visit. People went here and there in all directions, the inhabitants of various places decorated their streets and houses, all to no purpose, and of course much disappointment was felt. Yet, after all, it was scarcely to be expected that places near home would be neglected in favour of those at a distance.

There is a fine avenue of trees at Sandringham, and, as it is customary for every distinguished visitor to plant one, so of course the Queen must add one also, turning a sod deftly with a small carved spade kept for similar occasions. This is first on the programme for another day. East Newton church must be seen ; it is a nice drive to it just round the park. After that comes the " Home Farm." This is a favourite haunt of the Prince ; he is very fond of farming, and spends considerable sums of money in improving the land, and in the purchase of

machinery for that purpose. Close here is
the Working Men's Club. This club comes
in for strong approval of Her Majesty, and
very suitably after this she receives a deputation of the Prince's tenants, who present a
loyal address of welcome.

The sun is shining brightly, so everybody
drives to Dersingham and on to Snettisham,
a pretty seaside resort just getting fashionable. A local magnate is visited, and after
that the Queen goes to see a former retainer,
whose father, too, had been in the service of
the Prince Consort ; he is confined to his bed
with paralysis, and is doubtless much gratified
at this proof of appreciation of faithful
services.

The donkey carriage appears on the scene
next time Her Majesty goes out. The gardens
are first visited and duly admired ; after that
the stables, kennels, pheasantries, industrial
schools, &c. This takes the time up to
luncheon ; then they drive to Wolferton
church. Wolferton is a small village of
about forty houses ; the fact of the Royal

station being in the place has not made it
grow. The "Stud Farm" for hackneys is
visited, after that some cattle and cart-horses
at the bailiff's farm ; and a drive round the
village, to the intense delight of the cottagers,
who are, some of them, frantically waving their
husband's brightest and largest handkerchiefs
on clothes-props, while others are busy hanging
their table-covers out of window. " Is that the
Queen ? " says one youngster ; " why she is
only an old lady in black clothes ! Mrs. ——
looks a lot better than her when she's got her
Sunday things on." The fact being that Mrs.
—— wears brighter attire.

The Rectory is honoured by Her Majesty
taking tea there ; then they all drive home
to dine, and prepare for the grand event of
the evening — the performance of " The
Bells," and Trial Scene from the " Merchant
of Venice " by Henry Irving, Ellen Terry,
and company in the ball-room.

For some time active preparations had
been going on ; a small stage had been
erected, and scenery specially painted, &c.,

and everything was now ready for the performers, some sixty in number, to take possession. Tickets of invitation had been issued, and the county families in the immediate neighbourhood, together with the principal tenants and retainers, came up in full force. Many of the audience had never seen Ellen Terry and Henry Irving, so the excitement was great. It certainly was a very pretty sight when all were assembled, the decorations being very tasteful.

The Queen evidently fully enjoyed the performance, for although the hour was a very late one, her attention never flagged throughout. Those who imagine Royalty do not applaud ought to have been present on this occasion, for the applause from the Princes and Princesses was hearty and vigorous.

How the actors acquitted themselves it is not necessary to say, they are too well known. At the close, Her Majesty showed her appreciation by sending for the two principals, thanking them, and presenting to each a souvenir of the occasion, these souvenirs being still further supplemented by Her Royal Highness the Princess of Wales. Well satisfied were they to be thus honoured : I am sure that this hurried trip to the Prince's country residence will be a pleasant memory to each of them.

That was the last event of the Queen's visit ; for after an early luncheon the next day Sandringham was left behind, and Her Majesty once more drove to Wolferton, and there took leave of her son and his family, and ended a visit that from first to last was replete with interest.

CHAPTER XI

THE year 1889 was a memorable one for the Princess, for it was then that her Royal Highness saw her eldest daughter become the bride of His Grace the Duke of Fife.

It was on the 25th of June that the betrothal of her Royal Highness the Princess Louise of Wales to the Earl of Fife was made public. The announcement gave the most unbounded satisfaction to the country at large, and congratulations and presents poured in from every direction. So great were the number, and of such value were the gifts, that the total worth was computed at over half a million of money! The marriage was the outcome of a steadfast affection of nearly five years' duration, and every circumstance pointed to the mutual happiness of the affianced pair. On the 27th of July the wedding was duly solemnised at

THE DUCHESS OF FIFE
From a Photo. by W. & D. Downey

Buckingham Palace Chapel, in the presence of the Queen and Royal family and a large number of distinguished guests. At the wedding breakfast Her Majesty herself pro-

posed the health and happiness of the bride
and bridegroom, and in celebration of the
event the Earl of Fife was that day created
a Duke.

It seemed as though half the inhabitants
of London had squeezed themselves into
the spaces between Marlborough House and
Buckingham Palace, and it is difficult to say
who received the greatest ovation in passing,
the Princess of Wales, or the bride with her
father.

Her Royal Highness the Princess would
have the consolation of knowing her daughter
was marrying so that she could still see
very much of her, the Norfolk and London
residences of each being contiguous. Instead of a loss, there would be the gain
of a congenial spirit; the Duke being very
popular with all the family.

A gap was presently made in the Royal
circle by the departure of Prince Albert
Victor on an Indian tour; the remainder
of the family setting out for their annual
Danish re-union.

Soon after, two or three good causes were materially helped, such as the "Women's Hospital" in Euston Road, and the "Sama-

AT THE ROYAL NAVAL EXHIBITION, 1891
From a Photo. by Bedford Lemere

ritan Hospital" in Marylebone, by the presence of the Princess of Wales.

But so many charitable works have been undertaken by the Princess, that anything like a detailed account cannot possibly be given. That must be my excuse for omitting altogether what some may have considered prominent events. Early in May 1891 the Naval Exhibition was opened by Her Majesty, the Prince and Princess with other members of the family being present.

THE PRINCESS, 1892
From a Photo. by Russell & Sons

And I must now mention something of considerable importance—namely, the birth of the Princess's first grandchild in May. Her Royal Highness had the happiness of holding, in her arms the offspring of her own beloved daughter, and stood with the family group, met together to consecrate the infant to God's service.

Not many months after, Prince George was seized with a serious illness, for some time the issue being uncertain: untiringly and devotedly his mother nursed him, and at last she was rewarded with a prospect of his speedy recovery.

This brings me to a time when all the land rejoiced at the announcement of the projected marriage between the Duke of Clarence and the Princess May. No one was more pleased than the mother of the young prince; and, worn as she was with watching by the bedside of her younger son, the prospect of her eldest boy's happiness did much to sustain and cheer her.

Prince George became convalescent, and preparations commenced for the wedding of his brother. Congratulations poured in from all quarters; presents were arriving; committees were formed for organisation of suitable festivities; and already State programmes were being formulated, when suddenly came the intelligence that the bridegroom elect had been stricken down with influenza. Everybody sympathised, but few anticipated the fatal termination. Swiftly and remorselessly, however, the disease crept on; and presently all Europe was startled by the intelligence that Prince Albert Victor had passed away in the midst of his grief-stricken family.

Suddenly we were transported from joy and congratulation to mourning and sorrow. Muffled peals took the place of marriage bells ; and manifestations of grief, honest and true, came from every part of the globe for him who had been cut off in his youth—noble desires, worth scarcely known and appreciated, and a career full of promise prematurely closed.

The pathos of the event roused all the best feelings of the people, and every heart was stirred with the deepest pity for the bereaved parents, brother and sisters, august grandmother, and her who would so soon have been his chosen bride. Verily the torch of Hymen was quenched in tears, and behind the closed blinds of Sandringham and Osborne were hearts that could scarcely be comforted.

We "mourn with those who mourn " ; and although we knew comparatively little of the private life of the departed, we accepted the word of the Queen, whose whole life has been truth itself, when she said that "his charming disposition and high character had endeared him to her since his childhood."

Men and women looked upon the family sorrow as their sorrow ; Court formality was forgotten ·for the time ; and the father and mother in their bereaved home, *not* the Prince and Princess in their Palace, were in the hearts of the people ; a responsive chord was touched in nations that spoke not our tongue and knew not our land ; and look where you would everywhere could be seen marks and heard words of honest grief. The situation was so terrible, the tragedy so great, that it moved the hardest hearts ; our great city was as though the grim messenger had entered every portal. Theatres and other places of amusement were closed and barred. Clubs and residences had drawn blinds ; while the streets were partially deserted ; those who were out, walking along with sad and thoughtful faces.

The young Prince was interred with impressive ceremony; but nothing was more strikingly pathetic than the service held in the little church at Sandringham, when the remains were removed from the house; and nothing was more sadly touching than the strains of the beautiful hymn: " Now the labourer's task is o'er—Lord, in Thy most gracious keeping, leave we now Thy servant sleeping." As its strains rose and fell, lips quivered as they sang, sobs were in their voices, and sorrow in their faces: for the " servant sleeping " was one who had lived his life among them, and, by his many kind and thoughtful acts, endeared himself to them. Grief too sacred for words was that of the family who knelt in the chancel; in their midst the remains of the beloved son and brother, covered with the Union Jack, and surrounded with flowers.

Very sad, and touchingly simple, was everything on the day of the funeral, so far as Sandringham was concerned. The tenants of the estate, the heads of departments, the

children of the schools, the labourers and
gamekeepers, all clustered there near the
little church; some of them, indeed, travelling up to Windsor to the after ceremony.
No hearse and plumes, or other trappings of
woe, were to be seen, although mourning
dress was general in the large assemblage
gathered together from the villages around.

A short service—quite private to the
family and household—was held; then the
coffin, with its beautiful cross of lilies of the
valley, placed thereon by the sorrowing
mother, and the dead officer's sword and
busby, was carried out by labourers and
placed on a gun carriage of the Royal Horse
Artillery, which was surrounded by an escort
of the same regiment.

In solemn silence the procession moved
off, through a concourse of uncovered heads
and pale weeping faces. Every man, woman
and child present had been accustomed to
seeing the deceased Prince come to and
fro amongst them; and it was no wonder
that all sorrowed for the young life cut

off, and for those whom he had left to mourn him.

If anything could add pathos to the pathetic, it was the sight of the Prince of Wales—evidently bowed down with grief— walking, with bent head, immediately behind the coffin, the whole distance to Wolferton. Three Royal carriages contained the Princess and her daughters, the Duchess of Teck and the Princess May ; retainers of every grade going before and behind ; while large numbers of the spectators fell into the rear of the procession, walking six abreast.

Of the journey to Windsor I will not speak, save to say that it occupied several hours ; and that at every point where it was known that it would pass, vast crowds were gathered together.

At the railway station, flowers and palms were in profusion, placed here instead of the usual funeral appointments ; and even the Royal carriages were horsed with greys !

Guns firing, bells pealing minute strokes ; the weird yet sweet strains of Chopin's

"Funeral March" mingled together; and the short yet imposing procession passed slowly between guards of honour, who lowered their crape bound banners and stood like statues with reversed arms and bowed heads. All the mourners walked, each clad in glittering uniform. Close behind the body walked the late Prince's favourite horse; then followed the Prince of Wales and Prince George, the latter looking really too ill for the ordeal.

Highly impressive was the closing ceremony in St. George's Chapel; and through nearly the whole of it, the grief-worn father knelt near the coffin, with his bowed head nearly touching the pall.

The last epilogue was the extremely touching letter to the nation from the bereaved parents.

"The Prince and Princess of Wales are anxious to express to Her Majesty's subjects, whether in the United Kingdom, in the Colonies, or in India, the sense of their deep gratitude for the universal feeling of sympathy manifested towards them at a time when they are overpowered at the terrible calamity which they have sustained in the loss of their beloved eldest son. If sympathy at such a moment is of any avail, the remembrance that their grief has been shared by all classes will be a lasting consolation to their sorrowing hearts, and, if possible, will make them more than ever attached to their dear country."

CHAPTER XII.

As might be expected, very little was seen of our Princess for a long time after her great loss ; indeed, so thoroughly prostrated was she with the blow, that change of scene was absolutely necessary. Various places on the Continent were visited, a protracted stay being made at Copenhagen. The Prince and Princess were there, in fact, at the time of the Golden Wedding of the King and Queen, but took no part in the public festivals, which were prolonged for an entire week.

Early in 1893, the family were again travelling, Rome being one of the places to which the Princess went, accompanied by her son, now the Duke of York. Meanwhile, Rumour had been busy coupling the names of the Duke of York and the Princess May together ; and at last, on the 23rd of March a public announcement was made of the actual betrothal.

The utmost satisfaction was evinced on

every hand, congratulations pouring in from all parts of the world. As the wedding-day approached, a veritable en-chanted land met the gaze of the many thou-sands who per-ambulated the streets to see

THE PRINCESS, 1893
From a Photo. by W. & D. Downey

the decorations. It is not an every-day occurrence for the only son of the Prince of Wales to get married, more especially to an English Princess, and one who is dear to the nation, not only for her amiability,

but because of her popular and kind-hearted mother.

London was literally full. Kings, Queens, Princes and Nobles, country cousins and foreigners ; all were here to join the distinguished inmates of the palaces and mansions, or to swell the crowds in the streets.

What did it matter to the people that a general holiday had not been proclaimed ? They voted it to themselves ; and many of them commenced it before the wedding-day by going to see the Princess May on her progress from White Lodge to Buckingham Palace.

Then there were continual arrivals from Continental Courts, one of the most important being the King and Queen of Denmark : these must all be met and enthusiastically greeted.

And last of all, our own beloved Queen was coming up from Windsor on the 5th ; and so away went the people in their thousands, and right from Paddington Station to the Palace the thoroughfares were so thronged as to be almost impassable.

That same day the Prince and Princess of Wales gave a garden party at Marlborough House, for which over two thousand invitations were issued. Everybody determined to see all they could of the coming and going of the guests, and so it was not surprising that traffic was all but paralysed in the neighbourhood.

The morning of the eventful day dawned, and all things were ready. The brightest of suns and the bluest of skies cheered our hearts as we rose. Our centre of commerce woke up and found itself beautiful ; for the most costly and elaborate preparations had been made on every hand. Flags were flying, bands playing, bells ringing, and citizens, countrymen, and visitors from other lands poured into the streets in their tens of thousands.

It is with the utmost difficulty I make my way to Buckingham Palace, to which place I am fortunate enough to be honoured with admission.

If the preparations are elaborate outside, they are a hundred-fold intensified here, and

ROYAL GERMAN CHAPEL, ST. JAMES'S

From a Photograph

one is dazzled and bewildered by the grandeur and glitter on every hand.

Gold sticks, silver sticks, black rods, equerries, pages, state footmen, and officials of every description hurry hither and thither, conveying orders and putting finishing touches wherever wanted. Just as I reach the lower corridor the bridal bouquets and flowers for the table "arrive, so I have an early and near glimpse of the

THE DUKE OF YORK
From a Photo. by W. & D. Downey

truly wondrous floral display. Hurrying on to the State dining-room, a scene of matchless splendour bursts upon the vision. Art and wealth combined have produced an effect that, once 'seen, will never fade from the mind. The tables are laid, and very attractive they are, the chief attraction on them being the wedding-cake—made at Windsor by Mr. Ponder, the Queen's confectioner.

PRINCESS MAY
From a Photo. by W. & D. Downey

This room is prepared solely for the Royal Family and their Royal visitors, the ballroom being prepared for invited guests, and very beautiful it looks, the flowers and display of Her Majesty's plate being *more* than magnificent.

"A veritable fairyland," said one; "I never imagined anything so beautiful on earth," said another; and so remarks of wonder and delight went round, as one sight of inde-

scribable grandeur after another burst upon
us. It may seem enthusiasm on my part to
you who sit quietly and read these lines ; but
no words could convey the effect on those
who witnessed it, and no words could describe the stately beauty of the place.
The flowers alone must have cost a fortune ; everywhere you turned they smiled
back 'at you in their gayest and sweetest
manner.

The Bow Library is to-day prepared for
the assemblage of the Royal Family and
Royal guests, and demands a hurried glance :
thence to the Bow Saloon, where the register
will be signed by Her Majesty the Queen, the
bride and bridegroom, and the principal
Royal visitors.

But time is passing, guests will soon arrive ; so I take up my position at one of
the windows looking out on to the inner
quadrangle. Here everything is in active
preparation. State carriages are rapidly
driving in, the guard of honour, carrying the
Queen's colours, march in to the strains of

their magnificent band, and the whole scene becomes strikingly picturesque.

Now Royalty commence to arrive, heralded by the cheers of the multitude without, and greeted with the Russian, Danish, and English national airs. At intervals of a few minutes arrivals are continuous; then additional interest suddenly is newly aroused, for the galloping of equerries to and fro, and the gradual nearing of the coaches to the porch of the grand entrance tell that the first procession is about to leave for St. James's Palace.

A few carriages of ladies and gentlemen-in-waiting, then we behold some princely members of foreign Royal houses, our "Commander of the Forces," children and grandchildren of Her Majesty, the King and Queen of Denmark, and the Czarewitch, the last-named bearing such a remarkable likeness to the bridegroom that it is no wonder that one was temporarily mistaken for the other as he stood on the steps while the King and Queen took their seats.

How pretty those of Her Majesty's grand-

CHAPEL ROYAL, ST. JAMES'S
From a Photo. by H. M. King

children who were bridesmaids looked as they came down to take their places, their dresses of white satin and silver lace trimming gleaming in the sunlight, moss-rose buds fastened on the bodices, and, with the elder ones, also in the hair. In their hands are charming bouquets composed of lilies of the valley, orchids, white roses, and cattleva mendeli tastefully intermingled.

The first procession has departed, and almost directly the second is in course of formation. Verily, Lord Carrington and his subordinates have a busy time of it. Here and there you see them in all the glory of their State dress, carrying formidable-looking blue papers, to which they, from time to time, refer. Not a single hitch occurs; every coach draws up in its allotted order, and everybody takes his or her appointed place with the least possible delay.

The Comptrollers pass out and take their seats; then comes the bridegroom, with his father and uncle. Remarkably gay and well he looks, as he takes his way to the Palace

N

of St. James's in his State carriage of glass;
and who would not, with such a bride awaiting him?

Now comes the culminating point : the
bride is about to start. Everybody cranes
his or her neck, and stands on tip-toe. I
throw dignity to the winds, and mount to the
window-seat for a better view ; and so behold
the Princess as she slowly comes down the
steps led by her loving father, her eldest
brother slightly in the rear watching her
every movement with looks of affection.
Beautiful she looks, as she stands for one
moment, clad in silver and white brocade
trimmed with Honiton lace, and wearing the
Honiton veil worn by her mother years ago
when she plighted her troth to her handsome
husband in the little church at Kew, where
she was, as she said, married amongst her
own people. Tall and graceful, with com-
plexion and eyes of rare beauty, and an
expression of quiet thoughtfulness, but
brightened with happiness, the Princess May
is an ideal bride ; and as she bestows a

momentary caress on her magnificent bouquet
of white roses, orchids, lilies, myrtle, and
orange-blossom, I can come to the conclu-
sion that even were she a stranger in a
strange land, one look at her would secure
the affections of the people who are waiting
for her.

After the bride's departure there is a pause
of a few minutes; a coach of greater splendour than any that have preceded it, drawn
by four cream-coloured horses in the handsome trappings peculiar to them, draws up
under the porch, and in breathless expectation we await the coming of Her Majesty.
Presently the band strikes up the National
Anthem, arms are smartly brought to the
"present," the Queen's colours are lowered,
and, on the top of the steps, appears the
right-beloved Queen of England and Empress
of India. To-day the Queen is attired in
black silk, trimmed with the Honiton lace
she wore at her wedding. Her Majesty
looks well and happy as she is carefully
assisted to her carriage by the Munshi Abdul

Karim, with her being her Royal Highness the Duchess of Teck, who looks truly regal in her rich attire of cream silk. The cortége sweeps through the gates, the multitude without greeting it with one mighty and prolonged ovation of cheering.

We are, as it were, "off duty" for the time being, and turn about with one consent to compare notes with each other, and tell each other "how fortunate we are to have got in." It is only a favoured few who have obtained the privilege, and we feel important accordingly. Said one, standing by me, "If I shut my eyes for a moment it all seems like a dream." So it did ; but, unlike dreams in general, a fadeless one.

Well, we amuse ourselves by wandering about corridors and vestibules, and exchanging notes of admiration, until the time of return. Then I obtain a position on a balcony in goodly company, and watch the bride and bridegroom drive in together amid the strains of the "Wedding March" from the Guards' band. We wave our handkerchiefs frantically; I verily believe we should shout, only the multitude outside are doing it for us. Then occurred one of the principal episodes of the day, when the Queen took the Duke and Duchess of York on to the balcony, and thus presented them to her loyal people. Is it any wonder that cheer upon cheer rent the air, that the huge crowd manifested their delight in demonstrative fashion, and that the Queen was evidently pleased and gratified, and the bride almost overcome with such a continuity of affectionate welcome?

This over, the Queen, her family, and the guests, withdrew for the signing of the book specially kept by her for christenings and weddings; after that, proceeding to the state dining-room for breakfast, which meal was partaken of to the strains of music from the Scots Guards, stationed on the lawn below. The invited guests proceeded to their allotted rooms for the same purpose, and very merry was the feast. Right royal was the hospitality, and right hearty were the good wishes for the bride and bridegroom given in a variety of languages, but with a unanimity of purpose. A wedding is a wedding all the world over ; and when I tell you we celebrated it with due honour and joy, you may understand it was to us a gala-day supreme.

There is still another event to be witnessed, though, so once more I return to the balcony, there to witness the departure for Sandringham. Waiting for the starting, I am presently gratified by the King and Queen of Denmark, with the Princess of Wales and her daughters, passing along the corridor from which the balcony whereon I am standing is approached. Quite close to me are their Majesties, their daughter and her children, and I have ample time to note the handsome and well-preserved King and Queen, and the glow of returning health and happiness on the face of our beloved Princess.

A pause. Then more equerries walking backwards ; it is the bride and bridegroom on their way down to the carriage awaiting them. Graciously they bow and smile in answer to our bow and curtesy; and radiantly happy they each look.

Now I turn my attention to the inner quadrangle below, where princes, princesses, lords and ladies are taking up an outside position armed with satin slippers and rice. The open carriage, with its postillions in royal blue and red, draws up to the entrance; the Duke and his newly made Duchess appear on the steps; the shower of slippers and rice begins, fairly raining upon the happy pair as they take their seats. Then comes a touch of nature and fun that makes us all kin to-day. The Duke of Cambridge, the Prince of Wales, with his brothers and nephews, put their dignity of station in the background; ladies follow suit, and they all run across the quadrangle, some in front of the carriage, some at the sides, and some in the rear. Anyhow, they all mean to have a last look from the outer quadrangle; and little care they that they step into small puddles of the lately watered ground, to the

soiling of patents and satin. Now the
Princess May looks up to the inside balcony,
and then touches her husband's arm, and
causes him to look in the same direction.
There sits the Duchess of Teck, alternately
waving her handkerchief to her daughter,
and drying her tears with it. The Duke
of York takes off his hat, the Duchess throws
kisses to her mother, the band plays " Auld
Lang Syne," and the carriage recedes from
view under the archway.

The Duke and Duchess of York have set
out on life's voyage together.

God bless them, and bring them to a fair
haven.

It is hardly necessary to dilate on the
reception which awaited them outside from
the general public. Vast numbers of the
crowd had been waiting in their places almost
from sunrise, having made up their minds
to see at any cost. From one end of the
route to the other, it was one continuous
round of cheering, and one glitter of decoration. Triumphal arches, Venetian masts,

mottoes, flags ; and, above all, a perfect wealth of evergreens and flowers—red and white roses predominant—presented such a wonderful effect as surely few of us have ever before witnessed.

Then the bells rang, bands played, guns fired, and children from schools sang ; and altogether, it was a scene of enthusiasm that had never been equalled since the triumphant entry of Alexandra, Princess of Denmark, in March 1863.

CHAPTER XIII

THE wedding was the last event of a brilliant season; and very soon after the Princess and her two daughters turned their faces once more to Denmark; the Princess much enjoying the re-union at Fredensborg, where she spent a good deal of her time in painting and music. Her sister, the Empress of Russia, was also there, and the four Royal ladies being all good musicians, and the Queen of Denmark a first-rate harpist, harp and piano, duets, quartets, and eight-handed duets for piano were indulged in.

The enjoyment of the family party was, however, marred by the death of an uncle of the Princess, Prince William of Glücksburg, brother of the King; but the Princess returned to England benefited in her health, and much cheered in her spirits.

Early in 1894 we find Her Royal Highness taking her old place amongst us, striving —for the public good—to sink her own sorrow, to take her position in society, and to once again grace with her presence charitable and philanthropical events.

In May she represented the Queen at a Drawing-room ; the first she had held since 1891. The Whitsuntide sports at Sandringham were attended, to the great joy of the tenants and labourers ; and the Prince and Princess were both present at the annual drill of the London School Board at the Albert Hall.

The Welsh National Eisteddfod was visited ; and the Tower Bridge was opened amidst the loyal demonstration of tens of thousands of citizens : a loyalty displayed in the wealth of decoration quite as much as in the hearty acclamations.

The great event of the summer, however, was the birth of a son to the Duke and

Duchess of York on June 23, an heir in direct succession to England's throne. This was another link in the chain that binds our Royal family and the English people together, and once again was there universal joy. Both the birth and the christening took place at White Lodge, the charmingly pretty and essentially homely home of the happy young mother; the christening was in the presence of the Queen, the Prince and Princess, and many others of the family.

The present Czar—then the Czarewitch— had been to England on a visit to the Queen, and also with the Prince and Princess at Sandringham; and later on the Princess was with her sister in Russia; the first time since 1874. Her Royal Highness was also in Copenhagen for her eldest brother's silver wedding, and spent some happy hours at the Château of Bernstoff.

Scotland was the next scene, but the stay was brief; the Princess being so anxious about her sister in Russia, that she determined to be in England should her fears

of bad news be confirmed : thus shortening
her probable journey.

As all the world knows, the worst happened,
and Her Royal Highness set forth on a
sorrowful journey, only to be met half-way
with the news that she was too late to
see her Imperial brother-in-law again. Of
the great comfort her presence must have
been to her sister in her bitter trial I can
give but a slight idea. The tenderest affection has always existed between them, and
as I pen these lines our Princess is still with
her widowed sister to cheer and sustain her
in her need.

Although I have spoken at some length on
what England's Princess has done for the
people, not every one can imagine the *real*
value of her thirty odd years of noble self-
sacrifice. The Princess really works very
hard ; what she has done for years for
English society, and how she has preserved
it from the thorough stagnation that would
otherwise have overtaken it, with a Queen
who seldom, from age and other causes,

appears in the midst of her loyal subjects, is beyond conception. Her Royal Highness has had a very trying position to fill; no one could have filled it so well, for she is a Queen in all but name.

In town, during the season, engagements are so numerous that the Princess scarcely has an uninterrupted hour, and sometimes it is nearly as bad at Sandringham.

To " England's Princess " is due the becoming style of the dress of the present age, and the increased favour which the home manufactures have found with society.

Not only as Princess has she worked for the people, but as wife and mother she has set the noblest of examples; as wife she has been ever ready to assist her husband in all good works, and has been to the Prince what every woman should be to her husband—a loyal help-mate.

As mother, none have excelled her. Not only has she taken care that her children have had the teaching of the most able instructors,

but she has also personally supervised their
education.   In like manner as she has herself

PRINCESSES VICTORIA AND MAUD
From a Photo. by W. & D. Downey.

acquired every accomplishment, so she has
caused the same to be imparted to her

daughters.   Should one show any special
talent, that talent has been carefully cultivated, and while each one excels in some
particular direction, there are possibly no
better informed ladies in England than the
daughters of the Prince and Princess of
Wales.   Whether in London, on the Continent, or at Sandringham, their education has
fitted them for society requirements, estate
duties or rural amusements.

Above all, the religious instruction of the
young Princesses had been carefully attended
to : a chaplain was specially appointed for the
office ; and frequently the Princess herself
took her daughters to the children's service
on Sunday afternoon, held in the church
where he officiated.   Beyond this, the
Princesses have had the example of a godly
life from their mother, a mother whose foot-
steps all hope to see them worthily follow.

The graces, charms, and amiability of
" England's Princess " are accepted implicitly
by the entire nation.   She is never called into
question as to the good taste of anything she

may do, by the most violent republican. She holds the same place in the hearts of the people that she ever did. She will continue to hold it so long as she live ; and in years to come, when we are no more, and others occupy the places we now fill, the goodness and beauty of " England's Princess " will be regarded with ever-increasing admiration, and the example of a life nobly spent will be as a shining light, illuminating all future periods of England's history.

o

CHAPTER I

VERY little is really known of the *private* life of the Princess of Wales ; for although Her Royal Highness's acquaintances are legion, her real friends are few. Just one or two apart from the family have for many years held a foremost place in her affections ; to them she has been faithful.

Reared in retirement, the Princess has followed an inclination tending in the same direction, so far as the numerous duties of her position would allow. At Marlborough House, State functions are exacting, and here visitors come and go in great numbers. Many readers will be able to recall with me the beautiful grounds, the scene of so many

brilliant assemblies ; or the handsomely
decorated drawing-room with its fine dimensions and its splendid supporting columns ;
or again, the dining-room with its fine paintings and priceless plate, and the Indian room
with its unique collection of arms and other
curios arrayed on its walls. But all will
be more interested in reading of Sandringham, a place of which many hear, but which
few see. Here Her Royal Highness finds a
real *home*, and there is not the slightest doubt
that this is quite the favourite residence with
the Princess. There may be divers reasons
for this ; one is, that the scenery and
surroundings so much remind the Princess of
the home of her childhood ; another may be,
that this is the nearest point to Danish shores;
and certainly another is its seclusion. " Far
from the busy haunt of man " may be fitly
applied to it, so quiet and retired is its
position.

It is not an ancient castle with tower and
moat, not a show place such as would charm
a merchant prince, but beautiful in its

simplicity, and attractive in its homeliness ; in brief, a happy English home, inhabited by a typical English family.   When there, State and its duties, society and its requirements, are relegated to the dim past and shadowy future.   The Prince is a country gentleman, deep in agriculture and the welfare of his tenantry ; the Princess and her daughters pass their time in visiting the schools, the poor and the sick ; working in their dairy or at their sketching, deep in artistic and useful needlework, or recruiting themselves with riding and walking exercise.

Sandringham House is about seven miles from King's Lynn, which is the nearest town ; so that the family are not subjected to the prying gaze of the curious.   They have not, however, the inconvenience of the long drive from the above named place.   On the estate, and about three miles from the house, is a little village called Wolferton ; it has but about forty houses, but it has a railway station. To this station, in 1883, the Prince added a suite of Royal waiting-rooms, the addition consisting of a large entrance hall, approached by a covered carriage-way, with rooms on either side for the Prince and Princess. These apartments are handsomely and tastefully furnished, and are used not only as waiting-rooms, but occasionally for luncheon, when the Prince and his guests are shooting in the vicinity of Wolferton. The station lies in a charming valley, and, emerging from its grounds, you have before you a picturesque drive along a well gravelled road bordered with velvety turf, and backed with fir, laurel, pine, and gorse.

Rabbits in hundreds are popping hither and thither, pheasants are flying over your head, squirrels are scampering up and down trees; there are sounds of many feathery songsters in the branches; while, if you pause awhile, you may catch the distant murmur of the sea: certainly you can feel its breezes. You seem to get the beauty of the Highlands, the grandeur of the ocean, and the very pick of English scenery, all in one extensive panorama. The way lies all uphill, and having attained the heights, the view is beyond description, and gives an uninterrupted outlook over the North Sea, and a general survey of extensive range. On fine days, the steeple or tower of Boston Church (commonly called Boston Stump) can be plainly seen.

Proceeding on your way, you pass the park boundary wall, the residence of the comptroller, the Rectory, the little church of St. Mary Magdalene—with its flag waving in the breeze, denoting the family are in residence—take a sudden curve in the road, and find yourself in front of the Norwich gates, admitting to the principal entrance. One solitary policeman is here on guard, but he knows his business, and knows every member of the household by sight. His duty merely consists in opening and shutting the gates; but you may be quite sure he will not open to the wrong one.

These gates are worthy of more than a passing glance, for they are a veritable masterpiece of design and mechanism. They were in fact one of the features of the 1862 Exhibition, and were afterwards presented to the Prince by the county of Norwich. On the top is the golden crown, supported by the Prince's feathers. Underneath, held by bronzed griffins, are heraldic shields representing the various titles of the Prince, while the remainder is composed of flowers, sprays and creeping vines. They are connected with the palisading by rose, shamrock and thistle.

Although this is the chief entrance, it is necessary to proceed up the avenue and diverge to the left before the front of the building comes into view; then it will be seen to be of modernised Elizabethan architecture, with an exterior of brick and Ketton-stone dressing. Over the door is a carved inscription as follows: " This house was built by Albert Edward Prince of Wales, and Alexandra his wife, in the year of our Lord 1870." As a matter of fact, the estate had been purchased some nine years previous to that date, for a sum of £220,000; but the

old Manor House which formerly stood here
was in such a condition that, after vainly
trying to patch it up and add to it, it was
found desirable to pull it all down and build
an entirely new residence. It was not only
however the mansion that needed rebuilding,
but also the cottages of the tenants and
labourers; and much to the honour of the
Prince and Princess, these cottages were
their first care, and were all rebuilt and
several new ones erected before they took
possession of their own home.

The building is as nearly fire-proof as it is
possible to make it : the flooring of lias-lime
concrete, and all the walls of great thickness,
the whole of the connecting girders being of
solid iron. Passing in by the principal
entrance, you find yourself in a spacious hall
or saloon, one of the chief features of which
is the rich and massive oak carving : this
carving also being continued up the staircase.
This saloon is of such dimensions, that it was
formerly used as the ball-room ; but in 1883
the Prince added a wing to the mansion,

THE DINING-ROOM, WITH TABLE SET FOR DINNER, SANDRINGHAM

From a Photo. by Bedford Lemere

which included a new ball-room, to be spoken of later on. There is a talkative cockatoo here, which will immediately claim your attention with his shrill and repeated cries of "Three cheers for the Queen," which he continues without cessation until he is noticed.

Assume for the time being that you are a visitor by invitation at this beautiful home; you have been received in the saloon, just having time to glance at the paintings, statuary, palms and flowers. Perhaps you have taken a cup of tea there, after which you are conducted to the suite of rooms set apart for you. Dinner is at 7.30, but every clock at Sandringham is kept half an hour fast; the Prince, a most punctual man, has this method of bringing every one up to time. After meeting in one of the drawing-rooms, you proceed in the midst of the distinguished gathering to the grand dining-room, where the meal is served in state, although perhaps not with the same amount of formality you may be expecting. Your host and hostess

are so very affable, and have such a happy
gift of putting every one at ease with whom
they come in contact, that you insensibly
forget their august position, and find yourself
chatting with comfort and enjoyment. This
dining-room is of magnificent proportions,
and is hung with priceless Spanish tapestries,
the gift of his late Majesty the King of
Spain. There is a very costly display of
plate, much of which has been presentation.
The Prince and Princess face each other on
either side of an oblong table ; conversation
thus being easy. The decorations of the
room—of very rich and elegant design—are
particularly striking on the ceiling and supporting columns. The floor is of polished
oak, scattered with costly Turkish rugs.

After dinner you presently adjourn to the
drawing-rooms, of which there are a suite
of smaller in addition to the large one ;
these are all connected with the entrance
saloon by a broad corridor, which is ornamented with pieces of armour, antique china,
and other curios, with a plentiful selection of

THE DRAWING-ROOM, SANDRINGHAM

From a Photo. by Radford Lemere

palms and ferns. The large drawing-room is of beautiful construction, and fitted with windows reaching from ceiling to floor ; the walls are panelled with pink and blue, with mouldings of gold and cream. The furniture is upholstered in pale blue, with threads of deep crimson and gold ; the hangings are of rich chenille ; the floor of parqueterie, with a distribution of rich Indian rugs. In the very centre of the room is a large piece of rock-work with a tasteful arrangement (carried out by the Princess herself) of choice ferns and beautiful roses in bloom, while rising out of the midst is a marble figure of Venus. The fine Grand in an ebonised case is by Steinway. A plentiful scattering of music and books gives it a home-like appearance ; while hand-embroidery, sketches, painting on china, and feather screens show the variety of talent and skill of the ladies of the family. Also, as in each Royal house that I have visited, another feature is the very large number of photographs to be seen everywhere.

The Princess of Wales and her daughters
are all skilful and cultivated musicians, the
Princess herself excelling in this direction.
Then there may be skilled musicians amongst
the company; in any case, you are sure to
have some music, varied occasionally with a
carpet dance, tableaux vivants; or, if in the
case of gentlemen who prefer other amusements, there is the billiard-room, the Ameri-
can bowling-alley, or the smoking-room. In
addition, of course there are the libraries,
conservatories, with terraces and gardens
for summer evenings. A peep at the
"Serapis" room will interest you greatly.
It is half library and half smoking-room;
in it you will see the entire fittings of the
cabin the Prince occupied on his journey to
India in the vessel of the above name.

Breakfast is served at nine o'clock in the
morning, but the Prince and Princess generally take theirs in their private apartments.
Afterwards perhaps you have your correspondence to see to, and here I may remark
on the first-rate postal arrangements. There

THE CONSERVATORY, SANDRINGHAM

From a Photo. by Bedford Lemere

P

is a post office *inside* the house, which is also a money order office. Three deliveries per day come in that way, while mounted men meet the trains at Wolferton Station. There is also telegraphic communication with Central London, King's Lynn, and Marlborough House; and telephone to Wolferton Station, His Royal Highness's agent, the stud farm, and the bailiff.

Before proceeding to outdoor sights— which will not be possible very early, as your host has a multiplicity of business to get through—you had better take the opportunity of seeing some of the rare and beautiful treasures indoors. Of course every one is aware of the extensive travels of the Prince in many countries, and so will naturally expect to find many mementoes of the same in his home; but few, I think, will be prepared to find them so numerous and so valuable. Not only does one see them here and there in various directions, but one room of considerable dimensions is set apart altogether for their display, and an entire

day could be profitably spent in their inspection. It is not only their costliness and
beauty, but the associations which make
them of so much interest. Curios of all
sorts : from kings, princes, statesmen, civic
bodies, and celebrities of all shades and
denominations.

Perhaps, as a strong contrast to all this,
you may get a peep at the Prince's morning
room, which is usefully and plainly fitted
and furnished in light oak. There you will
see such a batch of correspondence that
you will be inclined to wonder when it will
be got through ; but the Prince is a capital
business man, and nothing is lost sight of.

The suite of libraries are well stocked with
English, French, and German literature,
many of which are presentation volumes in
handsome and unique bindings. In one of
these you will notice many reminders of
travel and sport in various climes.

The new ball-room is of immense size and
lofty construction, with fine bay windows at
either end and large alcoves on either side ;

THE BALL-ROOM, SANDRINGHAM

From a Photo. by Bedford Lemere

one of which contains a magnificent fire-place and the other windows. The walls are artistic triumphs, being finely painted in delicate colours ; and on them is arranged a splendid collection of Indian trophies. The floor is of oak, and kept in such a condition of polish as to be a pitfall and snare to any dancer not in constant practice. The band occupy a gallery at one end. If you should be at Sandringham when one of the annual balls take place, you are very fortunate. There are three of such—the County, the Tenants', and the Servants', the first of course bringing the *élite*. The tenants, I may say, are allowed to introduce a limited number of friends, a privilege highly valued and much sought after by the most remote acquaintance of each and every one living on the estate. Perhaps the servants' ball is as pretty a sight as one could desire to see in the room. The toilettes of the Royal Family and their visitors, the rich State liveries of the footmen, the scattering of Highland costumes, the green and buff of the gamekeepers, and the caps of the maidservants, all blending into an ever-moving kaleidoscope, picturesque in the extreme.

Few that are familiar with Sandringham, can enter this room without thinking of the occasion when the proud and loving mother entered leaning on the arm of her eldest boy, on the day he attained his majority. The fairest and bravest of all England were there assembled to do him honour; and from all parts of the world happy returns and long life were wished for him whom all regarded as their future king.

When visitors are at Sandringham it is customary for one or more of the ladies to be summoned to join the Princess some time during the morning, Her Royal Highness generally receiving them in her boudoir. This is, as you may expect, a wonderfully pretty and artistic room, containing many interesting reminiscences of her Danish home and many charming little presents from her children and other members of the family. The pretty miniature upright grand which

THE PRINCESS OF WALES'S BOUDOIR, SANDRINGHAM

From a Photo. by Bedford Lemere

stands here occupies a very high place in the estimation of the Princess, having been a present from her daughters on her birthday in 1893. This was the same instrument as was used by Paderewski on his voyage to New York in 1892. It is in a real English walnut case, and was selected for the purpose by Signor Paoli Tosti, from the firm of Steinway & Sons.

The gentlemen visitors have perhaps been conducted by the Prince to the stables, kennels, Model Farm, or any other of the hundred and one sights of Sandringham. Of course every modern improvement is found in the stables ; it has boxes and stalls for about sixty horses, and beyond that is a smaller stable in green and white tiled interior, with silver ornamented stalls. This contains the pretty ponies driven by the Princess. In addition to these stables there is also a fine stud farm at Wolferton. Lovers of dogs will have a great treat inspecting the kennels, for there are animals from all parts of the world, —St. Bernard, Thibet, Newfoundland, Terrier,

Chinese Chow-chow, Dachshund, &c.   The
Home Farm is a special hobby of the Prince.
Lovers of farming on scientific principles will
here be gratified with seeing the result of
every possible experiment and known improvement ; and neither here, nor at the
bailiff's farm at Wolferton, is there any
scarcity of fine cattle, but every one knows
the keen interest the Prince has always taken
in cattle breeding.   The pineries, grape and
other houses, together with the kitchen-
garden must also receive a share of attention.

By this time the luncheon hour of 1.30 is
at hand, and at this function there is a possi-
bility of Their Royal Highnesses joining the
party ; but in any case, after that meal forces
are united, and the plans for the afternoon
having been previously made, all visitors will
meet in the saloon a few minutes before the
appointed hour, there to await their Royal
host and hostess and family.   Perhaps you
may emerge on to the west terrace, many of
the rooms opening on to it from French
windows or conservatories.   One of the first

things you notice is a Chinese joss-house, or temple, made of costly metal, guarded on either side by two huge granite lions from Japan ; each of these was a gift to the Prince from Admiral Keppel. From here you step direct into the west gardens, which are artistically and tastefully laid out ; they have a sort of semi-wildness in some parts, and a perfect wealth of shrubs and pines, with artificial rock-work, a cave, a rushing cascade, and much of semi-Alpine appearance, so that it is with difficulty you realise that you are not in another land.

Near by, is a famous row of trees, all of which are likely to become historical, for each one has been planted by some world-renowned individual. Every one has a small board with a neat inscription on, which shows the name of the planter and the date. Chiefly perhaps you will note those placed there respectively by Her Majesty the Queen and the Empress Frederick. The park itself is extensive, well stocked with deer, and has two or three lakes of considerable size, with accommodation for boating in the summer, and first-rate for skating in the winter. This latter pastime is often indulged in by torchlight, and a very picturesque sight it is ; the trees around being illuminated, and lights fixed to the chairs occupied by some of the ladies, and pushed by attendant cavaliers on skates. At such times, the villagers are allowed to assemble as onlookers, indeed there is not very much of outdoor amusement at Sandringham, and often indoor amusement too, from which the cottagers are excluded.

Now we turn our attention to the model dairy ; everything in this is carried out to perfection, but the preference must certainly be given to that owned by the Princess. It is a Swiss cottage, containing five rooms ; one of which is a pretty tea-room with charming specimens of hand-painted tiles, some sketches by herself and daughters, and models of some of her favourite animals. Here the Princess often dispenses afternoon tea to her friends, often, too, cutting bread and butter and cake with her own fair hands. The dairy itself is covered with tiles presented by the Prince; they are peacock-blue with motto "Ich dien," and rose, shamrock and thistle entwined; and were specially made for the purpose in Bombay. A marble counter runs round the room, and standing thereon are a number of porcelain-lined silver pans. Some wall brackets contain silver, terra-cotta, marble and china cows, calves, &c.; one or two specimens of painting on china by the Princess Louise, Duchess of Fife; and a mounted head of the Princess's pet cow, with silver plate containing list of prizes she won at various shows. This dairy is not kept entirely for show, for here the Princess and her daughters are often engaged in the art of butter-making, in which they are thoroughly proficient. Clad in aprons and sleeves they go through the entire process, turning out first-rate pats of the article.

I have already intimated that houses—with the exception of the cottages—are few and far between at Sandringham; such is the case, and each one is the home of some

official of the household. One very handsome residence is that of the Comptroller,
General Sir Dighton Probyn, V.C., and
another is that of the chaplain, the Rev.
Canon Hervey.

York Lodge stands round at the other
side of the Park ; it was formerly known as
'' Bachelor's Cottage,'' and was built by the
Prince for sleeping accommodation of members of visitors' suites, Sandringham not
being sufficiently capacious for the large
influx in addition to the family requirements.

When the Duke of York was married,
various alterations took place ; and the
building is still being enlarged by the addition of nurseries and domestic offices.

In the park, and reached by a footpath
leading from the Hall, and approached by
the lych-gate, stands the little church of
St. Mary Magdalene. It is in the Perpen-
dicular style, and of ancient date ; was
restored in 1835 by Lady Harriet Cowper,
and has been twice further restored and
embellished by His Royal Highness the

Prince. It has some half-dozen windows of Munich and stained glass, a font cover of Henry VII. period, and other things of note. Conspicuous is a monument, erected by the Prince, to the memory of the late Rev. G. Browne Moxon, former incumbent ; and another of the late Rev. W. L. Onslow, former tutor. Next you notice a beautifully executed marble head of one who is held in loving remembrance of all who knew her—her late Royal Highness the Princess Alice, Grand Duchess of Hesse. Another work of art placed in the church is a bust of the late Emperor Frederick of Germany. There is also a stained glass window to the memory of the infant son of the Prince and Princess, and a medallion to the Duke of Albany.

A very handsome brass lectern recalls the time when the thoughts and sympathies of all Europe, nay, all the civilised world, were centred on Sandringham. I allude to the never-to-be-forgotten illness of the Prince. This lectern was placed there as a thank-

offering by the Princess, and bears the
following inscription :

TO THE GLORY OF GOD
A THANK-OFFERING FOR HIS MERCY
14th DECEMBER, 1871
ALEXANDRA

When I was in trouble, I called upon
the Lord, and He heard me.

The space in the church is very limited,
seating only about one hundred persons.
The Royal family occupy open seats of
carved oak in the nave.

The organ and choir are at the rear of the
building ; the organ, by Willis, is of sweet
tone, and presided over by a very able
musician.   The complete change from the
stately pomp of our London church service
is remarkable ; the choir is composed of
school children, gardeners, and other men-
servants ; the singing, however, is really
good, the voices indicating careful tuition.

I have heard down there of a former
organist who was not a great musician, and,
in fact, was more at home in the village shop

SANDRINGHAM CHURCH

From a Photograph

of which he was the proprietor. Sunday
after Sunday he made the most awful mis-
takes, and, in consequence, was continually
warned of his probable dismissal. The
Princess, with her invariable kindness, had
been the cause of his staying so long as he
did ; but one Sunday the climax was reached,
and the Royal patience fairly exhausted.
Mr. Gladstone (then in office) was on a visit,
and his solemn, grim countenance, as he
stood in the church, quite frightened the
poor man, inasmuch as he lost his head completely. The organ left off in the chants,
persisted in playing in the prayers, and altogether acted in such an erratic manner, that
it was no wonder that anger was depicted on
one countenance, sorrow on another, and
amusement on a few of the more youthful
ones. The old institution had to give place
to a new one, and a repetition of such per-
formances was thus avoided.

Every Sunday morning sees the Prince
and Princess in regular and punctual attendance, an example which all visitors invariably

follow, retainers being present as a matter of course.

On leaving the building, you will doubtless pause and look round the peaceful " God's Acre." Simplicity is stamped on everything, there not being a single imposing monument there. Several stones have been erected by the Prince in memory of faithful servants of the household, and there are also several placed there by the former proprietors of the estate. But you will be most attracted to the resting-place of the third Royal son, whose burial here has been already mentioned.

The Sunday afternoon is spent quietly in the house and grounds ; then in the evening some may, perhaps, drive to West Newton or Wolferton church—the Prince, Princess and family often do—while others may prefer to stay in for music or reading.

CHAPTER II

A WALK round the estate will well repay you. Nowhere have I seen the poor cared for as they are here, and if I were asked to name a model estate, I should unhesitatingly say Sandringham. What has been accomplished there is wonderful; when the Prince took the place in 1861 it was a comparative wilderness; some efforts had been made by the former proprietor in the direction of a school and some model cottages, but very little of real benefit had been accomplished, and the general conditions of the poor were not of the best. About seventy cottages were built or rebuilt; they are in Gothic style, and every convenience may be found in them. They mostly consist of five large and well-ventilated rooms, with an outhouse in addition. There are front and back gardens to every house, altogether about a quarter of an acre of land. The tenants are, of course, in the employ of the Prince, and every inducement is given them to cultivate flowers and vegetables, a Horticultural Show being held in the park every summer, and money prizes given to the successful competitors. Plenty of time is afforded them for cultivation of garden products, as every labourer in the employ of the Prince has finished his day's work at 3 P.M. The rent of these cottages is £3 per annum ; one block, which is superior, having a rental of £4 ; and, as the wages of labourers on the estate are from 18s. to 23s. per week, they may be looked upon as being very comfortably circumstanced.

In the various villages are the club rooms for the men ; here they can meet and play at bagatelle and other games, smoke their pipes, read the papers and magazines taken in, and obtain refreshments at a cheap rate. The refreshments include ale, &c., which is served of first-rate quality, and in mode-rate quantities. The Prince believes in working-men's clubs in preference to public-houses, and it is a fact that there is *not a single public-house on the whole of his estate.* If anything in the way of wine or spirits is wanted in cases of illness, it can always be obtained at the respective vicarages, to-gether with orders for meat, coals, and other necessaries; the Prince annually placing a sum of money in the hands of the vicars to spend in the requirements of the poor.

In every way the working-man's day of rest is respected at Sandringham; no un-necessary work of any description is done on the estate, and no trains are run to the Royal station.

So much being done for the men, the wives are not forgotten. Annual prizes are given for the cleanest and best kept cottages. The women are visited in their homes, and the Princess—a true mother herself—is not above holding in her arms the child of a cottager, or tending to the wants of the

sick. Many a little dainty finds its way
to their homes, these often having been
made by the Princess and her daughters;
frequently too, the Princess will sit and
read to the afflicted, or cheer them by conversing with them.

The children also are well cared for. Besides the ordinary schools which the Prince
and Princess have established in each village,
there is a flourishing Technical School at
the Royal Mews, where they are taught
useful occupations. It is not at all uncommon for the Princesses to give practical
assistance in these schools; they often go
in and ask the children questions, and sometimes take classes.

When any Royal birthdays or other
festivals occur the poor share in the enjoyment; dinners or teas being provided
for them. Should the Prince and his visitors
be shooting, a share is sent to the cottagers.
In their domestic joys an interest is shown;
if the occasion is a wedding, useful and
suitable presents are sent, and many times

the ceremony has been graced by the presence of Her Royal Highness and her daughters.

At Christmas there is quite a general rejoicing; joints of beef and all sorts of good cheer are freely given. It is customary for the Prince and Princess, together with the family and visitors, all to go down to the building where the distribution is made, and very hearty wishes are given on either side for the usual " Happy Christmas."

I have often heard the question raised, when dwellings and the general welfare of the poor have been under discussion : What does the Prince of Wales, and those acting with him, know of the real wants and requirements of such? The best answer to this would be found on the estate at Sandringham.

An inspection of any of the villages will prove how good a landlord is His Royal Highness ; and not only on his own estate does he interest himself for the people's welfare, but the same kindly encouraging interest is extended to all.   I remember seeing a lad of the King's Lynn Grammar School leaving Sandringham House on one occasion, the proud and happy possessor of a gold medal which had just been presented to him by the Prince in the " Serapis " room.   The lad's heart was full, for his future king had shaken him cordially by the hand, congratulated him on being the best scholar of the year, and wished him every success in life.   The kindly words spoken to him that day will never be effaced from the boy's memory.   It is in little acts like this that the Prince is endearing himself to his future subjects, as well as in the more prominent duties he fulfils.

Good as patron, landlord, and master, those who really *know* His Royal Highness cannot speak of him in sufficiently appreciative terms.   To such the real devotion and affection for his wife and children is very apparent. His amiability and thoughtfulness for others are marked traits in his character ; and what he has done for the country's good is proverbial.

CHAPTER III

I COULD give you numbers of incidents showing the true kindness of the Princess to the poor around her gates, and, by way of illustration, I will relate a few.

On one occasion, one of the lads employed in the Royal stables fell dead from the horse he was riding ; not the result of any accident, but simply heart affection. His mother was a widow and in bad health, so the lad's funeral was paid for, his mother received a weekly pension, and she was sent to London to have competent medical advice, and a few weeks' sojourn in hospital. At the time of her bereavement, and for long afterwards, the Princess was in the habit of visiting her and reading to her. Another case of distress graciously relieved by Her Royal Highness is as follows : A workman on the estate had for some reason been dismissed from his situation, and not being able to pay his rent, had no alternative but to leave his house ; this prospect in view was very serious for the man, as he had a wife and young family dependent on him. The wife, driven to desperation, went one morning up to Sand-ringham House, and asked to see the Princess ; this was of course refused, but the woman begged so hard, that at length one of the principal ladies of the household came to her and inquired as to her errand. While she was laying the affair before this lady, Her Royal Highness—who was already · attired for a journey to London that day— happened to pass the room where she was ; and gathering from her sobs that she was in some trouble, immediately went in and in-quired what was the matter. The poor woman then told her tale of poverty and distress, and not to unsympathising ears. The Prin-cess at once caused a note to be written, to the effect that it was her wish that the man be at once re-instated at his work. She also gave the woman a sovereign, and as she was very evidently ill, gave orders that she be driven home. We may form an idea of how the woman felt on her homeward journey, and with what feelings she conveyed the tidings of her success to her husband.

Another true incident, of comparatively recent date, is deeply pathetic. It occurred some short time after the death of the Duke of Clarence. As all know, the Princess tried to hide her grief, which was shown only in her fading health and tender consideration for others. One day, while walking with one of her ladies in the lanes, she met an old woman weeping bitterly and tottering under a load of packages. On inquiry it appeared she was a carrier, and made her living by shopping and doing errands in the market town for the country people.

"But the weight is too heavy at your age," said the Princess.

"Yes, your're right, ma'am; I'll have to

give it up, and if I give it up I'll starve. Jack carried them for me—my boy, ma'am."

"And where is he now?"

"Jack? He's dead! Oh, he's dead," the old woman cried wildly.

The Princess, without a word, hurried on, drawing her veil over her face to hide her tears. A few days later a neat little cart and a stout donkey were brought to the old carrier's door. She now travels with them to and fro, making a comfortable living, and has never been told the rank of the friend who has tried to make her life easier for the sake of her dead boy.

As I have pointed out, the Princess is a familiar figure in the cottages ; and one day last winter she went to visit an old woman whom she found knitting a stocking.

"Ah," said the Princess, "you can't do the heel as fast as I can ;" and taking the stocking from the woman's hand she there and then knitted her the nattiest heel possible. The stocking has since remained in *status quo*, and treasured in a drawer with the needles just as the Princess left them.

A laughable incident occurred on one of the Royal birthdays. Her Royal Highness and her daughter were just returning from a walk, and noticed a group of children playing opposite the Norwich Gates. No doubt they were there partly hoping they might have the opportunity of getting into the tea always given. They had come from a part of Dersingham that was not on the Royal estate, so had no right to such admission. However, the Princess, who is very fond of children, crossed over to them, and pleasantly asked them if "they were going to the schoolroom by-and-by."

" Noa, feyther doan't work for t'Prince."

One or two were then asked "what their fathers did," and various answers were returned. One informed the Royal lady that his "feyther went a-cockaling"—*i.e.*, gathering cockles, &c., on the seashore. But the climax was reached when one of them naïvely said that his "feyther went

R

a-poaching." Hearty laughter, that could not be suppressed, greeted this announcement, and orders were given for all the group to be admitted to the children's feast. That youngster must be deserving of pity if he took a verbatim account of this interview home. The poaching would take place on the Prince's estate.

Of the unselfish desire of Her Royal Highness for the enjoyment of others the following will testify. In the adjacent villages very often concerts and dances are arranged amongst the tenantry, these being dependent in a great measure on the attendance of the Sandringham House servants. Of course they are planned, as far as possible, when the Prince may be in town for a few days, as there are then but few visitors, and so a better opportunity for servants getting away. Sometimes the Princess may patronise a concert herself, but in order that as many as possible of the retainers should go, and go in good time, Her Royal Highness will dispense with the dinner in the grand dining-room, and have an informal meal served on a tray in a sitting-room.

Another anecdote that I think may interest my readers I cannot refrain from giving. Of course it is quite understood that no indiscriminate presents are received by the Royal family ; but on this one particular occasion the Princess made a deviation. With true tact and gracious courtesy, she saw the occasion when the breach of a rule would afford sincere gratitude to a loyal though humble admirer. A working man, who was something of a poet, had written a book. He sent a copy to Her Royal Highness, accompanied by a letter, saying that the book was sent as a token of the esteem and affection in which Her Royal Highness was held by the class of people to which he belonged. The Princess not only accepted the book in the spirit in which it was offered, but with her own hand wrote her courteous thanks for the gift, her cordial wishes for his success, and in encouraging terms bade him go on and persevere. I have very little doubt that that letter is the most treasured possession of this poetic workman.

Of course, much of the Princess's time even at Sandringham is devoted to visitors, the place often being quite full of such, who go down in two sets; from Friday to Monday, or from Monday to Thursday. Unless the Prince is away there is a large amount of hospitality—or rather was, previous to the death of Prince Albert Victor. Since then, the family when in Norfolk have lived very quietly; the associations of the place have been too saddening. Now, however, the Prince and Princess are beginning to somewhat recover from their heavy bereavement, and Sandringham is once more opening its portals to the representatives of society.

The Princess, however, has always set home interests in a very foremost position, and no mother in all our country has excelled her in devotion to her children. She has ever watched over and guided them in their more youthful days, and when they grew up has always been ready with her sympathy and counsel. She has comforted them in their troubles, shared their joys; and interested herself in their pursuits. Quite lately, the daughters have taken up photography, so the mother devoted herself to it likewise, and now all three are expert operators. Indeed, the Princess has more than one tea-service with pretty views on each piece, copies of photographs she had previously taken on her travels. Often, too, the Princesses may be seen fishing together, sometimes at Virginia Water, but more especially in Scotland, where they have landed many a salmon. The Princess has one very handsome rod, which was a present, and cost over £40 to make. It has six joints in gold mounts, and is fitted with carved ivory stoppers on which are designed the Prince of Wales's feathers.

Her Royal Highness has of course other recreations and amusements, but I think music is really the chief; and her playing is so good, and her reading of the most difficult passages so quick, that I have heard of the very finest musicians being altogether nervous if they have been asked to join Her Royal Highness in a duet.

With regard to needlework abilities I have already told you something ; but I can give you no just idea of the various ways in which the talent is exercised, from all sorts of fancy articles for home use and to help bazaars, to petticoats and other useful articles for the poor ; the useful also embracing all sorts of knitted garments. Then they each paint and draw, transferring many a pretty piece of scenery to paper or canvas. They are good riders and skaters : are thorough cooks ; also they make bread as well as butter ; are practical housekeepers, and in short seem to know how to do nearly everything. In addition, they find time to look after their birds in the fine Sandringham aviary ; to pay frequent and regular visits to their pets in the kennels ; as well as to do a great deal amongst their flowers.

Here I may mention that the favourite flowers of the Princess are lilies of the valley, roses and orchids.

One thing is certain, no one member of the family has an idle moment; from rising to retiring, each and all are continually occupied.

It may perhaps strike you how very difficult a matter it has been for the Princess to be—in spite of her many State and social duties—so thoroughly domesticated as she ever has been.. There is very little doubt that this can only be the result of continual effort and much method. How much this example has stimulated many a young mother who fancied "Society" demanded the whole of her time, we never can tell; certain it is that neglected nurseries are not nearly so much in vogue now as they were before our Queen and Princess of Wales showed the people unmistakably that they did not intend to relegate the duties of motherhood to others.

It would be idle to try to assert that

the leaders of the Royal family are not copied. It is a fact patent to all that what they wear, their likes and dislikes, and everything connected with them, is assiduously imitated in all directions. Such being the case then, we may reasonably hope that pattern is taken of their virtues also, and that England is wiser and better for the leadership of those whose chief desire is the welfare of others.

Much as we have admired the Princess in her public life, yet it is in the midst of her home circle we like to think of her and picture her; where, as wife and mother, she has conscientiously, faithfully, and lovingly filled the place God intended all wives to fill.

And here we take leave of her, with the earnest hope that Alexandra, Princess of Wales, may be spared for many years to adorn the high position which she has ever so worthily filled.

Printed by BALLANTYNE, HANSON, & Co.
London and Edinburgh

.8, 9, 10, 11, Southampton Street, and
Exeter Street, Strand, W.C.

PUBLICATIONS OF

GEORGE NEWNES, Limited.

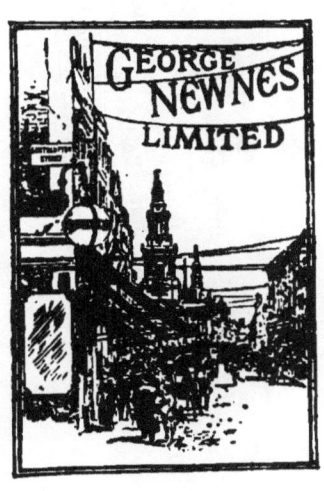

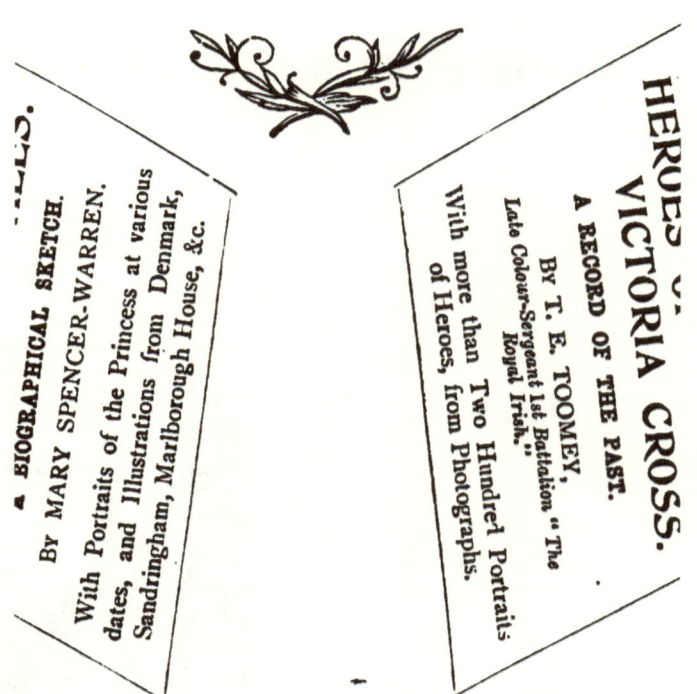

QUEEN VICTORIA'S DOLLS.

By FRANCES H. LOW.

With 40 Full-page Coloured Illustrations and numerous Sketches and Initial Letters, by ALAN WRIGHT. Handsomely bound in cloth and gold, with gilt Leaves.

Price 12s. 6d.

"A charmingly got up book, and most interesting."—*Truth.*

ZIG-ZAGS AT THE ZOO.

By ARTHUR MORRISON and J. A. SHEPHERD. 236 pp super royal 8vo, cloth extra, 7s. 6d.

"Every word of the Letterpress is readable, and there is no small amount of acute observation conveyed in the rambling remarks on various creatures' characteristics. It would be superfluous to praise or single out any particular drawing; but the bears, perhaps, show Mr. Shepherd's skill, and various birds his mastery of the art of suggestive caricature. *Zig-Zags at the Zoo* is a necessary volume to all people who are fond of animals and gifted with a sense of humour "—*Spectator.*

"A most delightful book."—*The Glasgow Herald.*

ILLUSTRATED INTERVIEWS.

By HARRY HOW. 320 pages, with 284 Illustrations, cloth gilt, gilt edges, 6s.

"Mr. Harry How has done an excellent thing in collecting and publishing in a handsome octavo his 'Illustrated Interviews' (17) with distinguished personages. There are seventeen articles. Among the more prominent of the men whom Mr. How has interviewed, and whose conversations as to themselves—their careers, habits, tastes, and so on—are here reproduced, are Cardinal Manning, Mr. Rider Haggard, Sir Frederick Leighton, Mr. Irving, Professor Blackie, Lord Wolseley, the Bishop of Ripon, Mr. Harry Furniss. These interviews are described in a crisp and most attractive style, and Mr. How has related what he has got to say in excellent taste. The illustrations are as interesting as they are numerous and well selected, and this is saying a great deal. They are produced in a manner that leaves nothing to be desired, and which greatly enhances the attractiveness of an already attractive and eminently readable volume of the 'Strand Library.' "—*The Glasgow Herald.*

"Mr. How always manages to tell us something interesting about his various victims, and those who desire to know all about the life and home of notable men and women of the day, like Mr. W. S. Gilbert, Sir Frederick Leighton, Dr. Russell, Mr. Henry Irving, Miss Ellen Terry, and others, can hardly do better than consult his graphic pages."—*The Daily Telegraph.*

POPULAR NOVELS.

In One Volume, price 3s. 6d. each.

Shafts from an Eastern Quiver.

By CHARLES J. MANSFORD. With 25 Illustrations by
Arthur Pearse.

"Mr. Mansford has the gift of a story-teller, and he uniformly writes
like a scholar. . . . . The illustrations, though small, are admirably
executed, and enhance the piquancy—though that was hardly needed—of
the letterpress."—*Spectator.*

"Will strike many a youngster with great delight."—*Daily Chronicle.*

The Beechcourt Mystery.

By CARLTON STRANGE.

"No one will begin the book without finishing it."—*Manchester Courier.*
"A novel and well constructed plot."—*Liverpool Courier.*

What's Bred in the Bone.

By GRANT ALLEN. Ninth Thousand.

The Sign of Four.

By A. CONAN DOYLE. Twenty-Second Thousand.

Hearts of Gold and Hearts of Steel.

By the late HENRY HERMAN. Second Thousand.

For God and the Czar.

A Story of Jewish Persecutions in Russia. By J. E.
MUDDOCK. Fifth Thousand.

Only a Woman's Heart.

The Story of a Woman's Love : A Woman's Sorrow.
By J. E. MUDDOCK. Second Thousand.

A BOOK FOR GIRLS.

Two Girls.

By AMY E. BLANCHARD. With Illustrations by
Ida Waugh.

"A delightful addition to the girls' bookshelf."—*Gentlewoman.*
"A bright sparkling story for girls, brimful of innocent fun."—
Liverpool Courier.

THE LIBRARY OF USEFUL STORIES.

Small 8vo, cloth, price 1s. each Volume, post free 1s. 2d.

I.
The Story of the Stars.

With 24 Illustrations. By G. F. CHAMBERS, F.R.A.S.,
Author of "Handbook of Descriptive and Practical
Astronomy," &c. [*Just Published.*

"Mr. Chambers writes in a vigorous and attractive style, and shows
himself able to combine to an uncommon degree scientific accuracy of
statement with a clear and attractive exposition. Beginners in astronomy
who wish to acquaint themselves merely with the outlines of a noble
science will find this volume of real service."—*Speaker.*

II.
The Story of Primitive Man.

With 88 Illustrations. By EDWARD CLODD, Author of
"The Story of Creation," &c. [*Just Ready.*

III.
The Story of the Plants.

With Illustrations. By GRANT ALLEN. [*Shortly.*

IV.
The Story of the Earth.

With Illustrations. By H. G. SEELEY, F.R.S., Professor of Geography in King's College, London.
[*In the Press.*

V.
The Story of the Solar System.

With Illustrations. By G. F. CHAMBERS, F.R.A.S.
[*In the Press.*

To be followed by other Volumes, of which due notice will be given.

The Rubies of Rajmar; or, Mr.
Charlecote's Daughters. *A Romance.* By Mrs.
EGERTON EASTWICK (Pleydell North). Crown 8vo,
cloth, 3s. 6d.   [*Just Ready.*

Stories from the Diary of a Doctor. By L. T.
MEADE and CHARLES HALIFAX, M.D., Authors of " The
Medicine Lady." With 24 Illustrations by A. PEARSE.
378 pp., crown 8vo, cloth extra, price 6s.

This volume contains Twelve Stories illustrative of the various
experiences met with during the professional career of a Medical Man in
large practice. They are not less striking than those told in Samuel
Warren's " Diary of a Late Physician," whilst several of them are
founded on actual occurrences, and others show the immense advances
which Medical Science has made in these later years.

" Cleverly-planned and brightly-told stories."—*Bradford Observer.*

The Romance of History. By HERBERT GREEN-
HOUGH SMITH. 292 pp., crown 8vo, cloth, 3s. 6d.

A series of graphic sketches of the leading incidents in the lives of
Masaniello, Prince Rupert, Marino Faliero, Bayard, Lithgow, Jacqueline
de Laguette, Vidocq, Lochiel, Casanova. The volume is printed on
antique paper, and bound in old style with uncut edges.

Castle Sombras: an Historical Romance. By
HERBERT GREENHOUGH SMITH. Crown 8vo, printed on
antique paper, cloth, old style, 2s. 6d.

" An historical romance of vital power and interest. . . . . The
dashing and splendid story of Captain Dare and his ideal love, of wit and
valour, and sheer devilry, would make a fine play."—*The World.*

" A very thrilling story . . . . the excitement continues to the
very last page."—*Academy.*

Memoirs of a Mother-in-Law. By GEORGE R.
SIMS. 6th Thousand. Cloth, 2s. 6d.; post free, 2s. 9d.

" This is a pleasant sample of ' Dagonet's ' semi-humorous writings.
He has a peculiar talent of finding amusement in experiences relating to
dwellings, servants, shopkeepers, tradespeople, and other folk connected
with the domestic household, and the ' Mother-in-Law ' in his new book
deals in a very masterful way with all the foregoing subjects, and many
more besides. The lady has a mind and way of her own, her mood is the
imperative, and what she says and does as guardian, not only of her own
but of her son-in-law's house, is spiritedly told by Mr. Sims, especially in
the earlier chapters."—*Freeman's Journal.*

"THAT MARVELLOUS DETECTIVE."

ADVENTURES OF SHERLOCK HOLMES.

By A. CONAN DOYLE.

324 pages, with 104 Illustrations by Sydney Paget.
Cloth extra, gilt leaves.

PRICE 6/-

Also a cheaper edition, crown 8vo, 3/6.

"For those to whom the good, honest, breathless detective story is dear, Dr. Doyle's book will prove a veritable godsend."—*Athenæum.*

MEMOIRS OF SHERLOCK HOLMES.

By A. CONAN DOYLE.

280 pages, with 92 Illustrations by Sydney Paget.
Cloth extra, gilt leaves.

PRICE 6/-

" Should become a favourite gift book."—*Liverpool Mercury.*

THE SIGN OF FOUR.

An earlier adventure of Sherlock Holmes.

By A. CONAN DOYLE.

Crown 8vo, cloth, 3/6.

"The 'Adventures of Sherlock Holmes' should be read by all who desire to improve their faculty of observation. Fathers would do well to make it a birthday present to their boys, and if they do this, they certainly may have the comforting thought that the book will be read from beginning to end."—*Glamorgan Gazette.*

BOUND VOLUMES OF WEEKLY
AND MONTHLY PERIODICALS.

Tit-Bits, from all the most interesting Books, Periodicals and Contributors in the World. [Vols. 1 to 27, 4to, cloth, 3s. 6d. each. Vols. 1, 2, 4, 5, 11, 19, and 20 out of print.]

The Strand Magazine. An Illustrated Magazine. Edited by GEORGE NEWNES. Vols. 1 to 8, cloth extra, gilt leaves. Price 6s. and 6s. 6d. each. [Vols. 1 and 2, 21s. each.]

The Picture Magazine. Vols. 1 to 4, each containing about 1,000 Pictures, cloth extra, gilt leaves, 6s.

Strand Novelettes. Vols. 1 and 2, each containing Thirteen Stories, with Illustrations, cloth extra, 2s. each.

6,000 Tit-bits of Curious Information. Being 6,000 Answers to 6,000 Questions from the Enquiry Column of *Tit-Bits,* in 6 vols., price 2s. 6d. each. [Vol. 1 out of print.]

. Each Volume complete in itself.

" Worthy of a place as a reference book in every library."—*Hygiene.*
" As throwing light on abstruse questions it would be hard to beat, and is not only useful but interesting."—*The Medical Times.*
" This is a wonderful book, ranging as it does over nearly the whole field of knowledge accessible to men. As a compendium of interesting and useful information this little book is surely for its size among the best that was ever produced. No library should be without a volume that deserves a place on its shelves, side by side with dictionaries, cyclopædias, concordances, and other books of reference."—*Scholastic Globe.*

SERIALS now in course of Publication.

The Strand Magazine, 6d. monthly.

The Strand Musical Magazine, 6d. monthly.

The Picture Magazine, 6d. monthly.

Round the World, 6d. fortnightly. To be completed in 12 parts.

Round the Coast, 6d. fortnightly. To be completed in 8 to 12 parts.

The Art Bible, 6d. monthly. To be completed in about 12 parts.

Strand Novelettes, 1d. weekly.

Tit-Bits, 1d. weekly.

www.ingramcontent.com/pod-product-compliance
Lightning Source LLC
Chambersburg PA
CBHW021047030726
47496CB00006B/1727